LOVE AND DEATH IN THE CITY OF BONE

A SCIENCE FICTION SHORT NOVEL

RAYMUND EICH

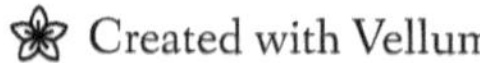 Created with Vellum

LOVE AND DEATH IN THE CITY OF BONE

Perhaps our only sickness is to desire a truth which we cannot bear rather than to rest content with the fictions we manufacture out of each other.
– Lawrence Durrell
Clea (*The Alexandria Quartet*, Book 4)

MY FOOTSTEPS ECHOED under the high ceiling of the spaceport's arrivals gate. Plastic shrouds wrapped all but one of the interview stations. At the last open interview station, the guard's frizzy hair and long ears reminded me of Nesbitt, Juliette's husband. I held out my ALECS passport and let the guard take a fingertip scraping and a retina scan to confirm my identity.

After a few seconds, the machine gonged and a green light glowed on its panel, sequencing of my DNA complete. The guard gestured at a gray plastic frame, two meters fifty tall, one meter fifty wide, thirty centimeters thick. Under the center of the frame, bee-striped lines marked the outlines of feet.

"Stand there until released," the guard said.

I raised an eyebrow at the frame, then at him. "Brain activity scanners are voluntary at any ALECS arrival or departure point."

"The rules have changed. Stand there until released."

He set his fists on his hips. The gesture set a crease into the ALECS patch on the guard's blue sleeve. Under the patch, no doubt, lay the logo of United Sodalities of the Galaxy, soon to be the only human organization allowed to remain on this planet. I could waste time with his superiors, arguing protocols they knew and disregarded, with little hope of evading the scanner. Or I could comply. In one inhalation I planned my thoughts, then did as he bade.

The guard moved around the frame and faced me. Motors spun up and fans whirred in the plastic frame as he scowled at my passport. "What's the purpose of your visit, *Mr. Lee?*"

I let slide his willful refusal to use my honorific. "The Way in the West has sent me to supervise the withdrawal of its personnel and assets from Elard, according to the Indigenous Autonomous Council's decree." A sense of purpose filled in behind my eyes. Sadness at our mission's end hung from it like icicles. He would expect the scanner to pick up both those feelings.

It helped I felt them.

His scowl shifted targets to my face. "Is that your sole purpose?"

"I might look up some old colleagues," I said. Stolen hours with Juliette returned from memory and touched my inner senses. The glow of afternoon sun flooding the opacity of the window near my narrow bed. The texture of her kisses. The grinding of our pelvises against each other. The public trysts, in her jitney, that one in the women's restroom at the café on Gregory Dialogus Street, sneaking out with disheveled hair and untucked shirts only to find Purcell waiting for us—

Mustn't think about Purcell—

"Step forward," the guard said. He snapped shut my passport and held it out, pinched between his thumb and forefinger. "Your papers are in order. I cannot deny you admittance. But here's some advice. The rules you might remember from your previous stay, when the ALECS administrators ruled the human settlement and the wishes of our native brethren were ignored, they've changed. The natives have decided your doctrines are false. We abide by those wishes. You'd be wise to do the same, Mr. Lee."

I took the passport from him, lifted my shoulders, and turned away. I had a month on Elard to learn her secrets. Secrets I had missed on my posting here decades prior.

The planet's secrets. Not Juliette's.

Outside the arrivals gate, a robotic flatbed cart waited with my suitcases. Its front structure bore shoulders and head, eyes level with my chest. A smile formed on its cartoonish features when I approached. "A jitney waits for you outside," it said.

I trickled my hands over the barely-visible seal in the uppermost suitcase. Cool to the touch. No sign of forced entry by the security guards. "Follow."

My heels clacked and the cart's tires whispered on the tile floor. I alone had arrived today. The only other sounds and motions on the concourse came from cleaning robots. Chairs and tables gleamed in the glow of lighted ceiling panels and waited for passengers never to come. A cleaning robot, the size of a tiny dog, clung on gecko-like feet to a poster saying *The United Sodalities of the Galaxy and the Indigenous Autonomous Council Welcome You to Elard*. A lighted strip in the frame above the poster glinted on the robot's carapace. With a raspy sound, the robot licked the face of the Sodalities's local operations director. An augmented reality server pushed his name to the video screens in my contact lenses. Vainqueur. A name I'd never heard before.

A dozen paces further, a light had burned out over a poster with the ALECS logo and an array of smiling humans diverse in race, sex, and attire. Their puffed hair and narrow, starched lapels resembled decades-old images of the four of us on the soft synthleather couches in a back corner of the café. *The Apostolic League of Earth Communities of Spirit. Many Manifestations, One Truth.* Thick lines of dust marked the edges of the poster frame.

I rounded a last corner and entered the spaceport atrium. My footsteps echoed off the concrete walls and vast front windows. My pace remained constant but my heart sped up. Across kilometers of scrubby desert, the human settlement thrust its bony fingers toward the sky.

The most important three years of my life had been spent in and around those living buildings and the wide boulevards between them. I had been a callow boy, deluded by my recent diploma and my accepted application for an extrasolar posting into believing I was a man.

Three years of fruitless missionary work humbled my naive certainty in both The Way in the West's teachings, and my own abilities to persuade the natives. *Alien Lifeforms Extremely Contemptuous of Salvation,* Purcell had said with his customary cynicism, and Nesbitt had narrowed his eyes.

A few months in Juliette's close orbit demolished my masculine pretense of control over my surroundings and my emotions.

She lived still among those bony towers.

The doors to the loading zone parted to reveal a single jitney waiting along a hundred meters of curb. On its side, the ALECS logo, the white sun of the Transcendent pouring out the rainbow-colored waves of the different spiritual communities. A standard vehicle from the motor pool. The baking air desiccated me, pulled recollections of field work out of the depths of my memory. I shaded my eyes and squinted at the cloudless sky under noontime Elar. Quick steps to the jitney, and I sagged into the rear seat before ordering the air conditioning vents to aim themselves at me. I stepped down the windows' opacity to give myself a sepia-tinged view of the spaceport and the landscape. Thumps came from the trunk as the robotic cart loaded my luggage.

Minutes later, the jitney hurried down the road toward the

human settlement. Straight as a crow's flight, the same low, mounded median of rocky soil and sparse Terran shrubs divided the two inbound lanes from the two outer. To the sides, new boundary fences ran parallel to the road, ten meters from the paved edges of the shoulders. Atop the barbed wire, concertina coils angled toward the road. In the old days, the ALECS concession stretched five kilometers to either side, marked by a fence a person could climb. Beyond the fences, rocky desert tufted by a few Elardian plants stretched to the edges of the plateau. The natives rarely strayed this far and high from the great narrow sea stretching halfway around the planet.

My thoughts turned to the hidden one of my purposes. Three days before I left Earth, my superiors sent me to Prague, where I met the executive committee of The Unneeded Hypothesis, Purcell's sponsors.

We never learned his fate on Elard. In the decades since he disappeared, our leadership focused on more urgent matters. But our stature declined anyway, and our number of adherents has shrunk. Learning Purcell's fate would be one of the last victories we could win. Now that the United Sodalities of the Galaxy has cajoled the natives into expelling the rest of us, our chance at even that victory is slipping away.

Three kilometers outside the window, across a city of midrise apartment buildings housing tens of thousands living mostly in virtual reality, gray-bellied clouds brushed the spires of St. Vitus' Cathedral. *Where do I come in?* I asked.

The executive winced. *We can't afford to send an agent to Elard. Your superiors in Calgary agreed we could partially fund your trip if you do this for us.*

Calgary didn't tell me—

His eyes grew imploring. *We ask for a pair of reasons. First, yes, our spiritual paths differ, but they are more consonant than any others. We both strive to see the universe as it is, yes? Unlike the USG, and the Universal Church of Christ, both telling pretty lies of the universe as it could be, if only the masses would bow down to the USG's historical dialectic, or the UCC's god.*

All that is true. I knew the answer before I asked my next question. *And the other reason?*

In his reports, Purcell called you his friend.

A sign announced a thousand meters to the settlement's gate. To the left, beyond the road's outbound lanes, the boundary fence turned a right angle away from the road. The airfield looked little changed. The aircraft hangar and liftpad were as I remembered, shimmering in the heat. No one was about, and on a pole near the hangar slumped the ALECS flag.

Between the airfield and the settlement, a few jitneys rolled over rock and packed sand between several new buildings. Extruded like giant sausages, only narrow, translucent windows and recessed doors broke up their smooth shells. Near each door was a building number and the spiral-galaxy-and-all-seeing-eye logo of USG.

The jitney slowed for a sallyport arcing over the inbound lanes. A curtain of air buffeted it and it stopped under the sallyport's shade. A guard tapped the window and I told the jitney to open it. "Yes?"

He leaned his head in and slid off his sunglasses. A speaker bud like a white chrysalis showed in his left ear, and flesh-toned discs on the sides of his Adam's apple marked his subvocal microphones. "Traffic control verification. Your destination?"

"The Way in the West, Elard Headquarters, 14 Laozi Street."

"Thank you." He angled his head to his left and got a faraway look, listening to his earbud. "May your stay be productive. Good day."

The jitney rolled forward, through another air curtain, and back into the glare of Elard at midday. Dark shadings and the outlines of pried-off letters marked shut-down shops along Guru Nanak Boulevard. A few remained open under unfamiliar names. Harvard Square Poetry Slam, Portland's Finest Coffee, Park Slope Brewery & Pub Grub. All had windows tinted against the harsh light. The boulevard lacked any traffic other than me.

A few minutes later, I arrived at our headquarters. A glimpse up the front facade showed little change in the three floors of white bone and reflective windows. Our banner hung slack above the vehicle entrance. The banner bore the *taijitu*, its light side shaped roughly like the Americas. I turned into the parking garage entrance and shade swallowed the jitney.

I climbed out near double glass doors leading into the building. Though attenuated by the garage structure, Elar's glare still forced me to shield my eyes with my hand to widen my pupils enough for the retina scanner mounted on the wall. I pressed the thumbprint scanner and said, "Darren Lee, *daoshi* of the third rank."

The doors shuddered as the magnetic seals gave way.

I went in, savored the cold air thick like a hotel's, and followed a virtual arrow to the elevator. It debouched me on the top floor.

Silence reigned throughout the floor, broken only by a few low voices at the far end of a cubicle layout. Beyond the voices, lights glowed in one of the offices around the perimeter. I presumed the lighted office belonged to Scobee, the director of local operations. Between the elevator and the voices, the cubicles stood empty save for a few empty snack wrappers and abandoned datachips in their back corners and deep in their footwells.

In his office, Scobee stood behind his desk, arms crossed behind his back, shoulders high and rigid. His right eye drooped, and both eyes had heavy bags. I waited in the open doorway until he greeted me. "Welcome—back—to Elard, *Daoshi* Lee."

"You seem displeased to see me."

A moment of alarm flashed wide his eyes. "No, *Daoshi*, certainly not. The chance to meet and share the Way with a *daoshi* of the third rank, I can only be pleased—"

"Perhaps *you* can, but what about all the other parts of your psyche?"

"They, yes, they are pleased to. I—part of me, rather—wonders, though, why Calgary sent you. And without warning, that's what puzzles—me." He cleared his throat. "My reports to Calgary have made clear our evacuation is on schedule. Haven't they?"

"I can't speak for Calgary, but they must see it differently. After all, they ordered me here."

"We'll be down to ten percent of our complement when the ship that brought you takes off. There are only four remote sites left and I shouldn't have any more trouble shutting them down—"

"Brambles in the path."

For all our claims of relying on inner wisdom, we regurgitate our share of mantras. *Brambles in the path? Go around them. That's all you need. Don't bother asking, 'why are such things made in this world?'*

Scobee's head jittered, then stopped. "Of course, Marcus Aurelius said it so well, and so long ago." His shoulders slumped. "*Daoshi,* I'm sorry, all the difficulties in wrapping up our presence here are getting to me. I've been doing well closing down our operations, and still Calgary doubts me...."

"The handbook on withdrawing a mission from an alien planet was all theoretical," I said, tone chummy, "until now. Mind if I sit?"

He nodded, gestured at a chair facing his desk. He dropped into his. "The handbook came close enough. I've had to cut a few corners —I think my results will show those were good decisions—"

"I'm sure they will. Yet even if the handbook gave your team good advice, the logistics of packing up our facilities and shipping out hundreds of people must have kept you up at night."

"The logistics are just details. We're on top of them." He back-handed the air, confident and nonchalant, but his hand soon fell to the glass desktop. A dour look filled his face and he retreated deeper into his chair. "The United Sodalities is the difficulty."

"How so? USG won over the vast majority of the natives; the natives ordered the rest of us to leave. What am I missing?"

He looked haggard for a moment. "You know those aren't ALECS security personnel at the spaceport and the settlement gate."

"Yes. So? USG security is running a victory lap." I peered at him. "Have they interfered with your operations?"

He rocked his chair back and forth in a slow but agitated tempo. "Not directly. Yet. Much. Mostly they just watch and jump on our every transgression. Did you see where our logo used to be on the building? No, of course not, it's on the side away from the street."

His window faced the same direction. I stood, went to it. The next block held dogtrot stucco houses where married ALECS personnel with families had lived. Beyond lay forty meters of bare dirt, then a barbed wire fence marked the settlement perimeter. Hazy with distance and heat shimmer, past the canyon-carved edge of the plateau, close to the sinuous indigo sea, thick brown piles marked the nearest native villages. "Facing the lowlands," I said. "Visible to the natives. If someone gave the natives a pair of binoculars."

"Exactly. Visible enough to offend their newfound faith in USG-ism, at any rate. We wasted two days covering up the logo and spreading osteoclastic factors to get the building to slough it off."

"At least it was only two days."

Scobee shook his head. "They forbid access to some of our old field posts. They're uncrewed, we scrubbed anything sensitive when our people last left them, so maybe it doesn't matter, but the handbook says we should double-check those sites and remove anything which might affirm our tradition." He looked at me for approval.

Purcell's unoccupied airmobile had been found in the high desert two hundred kilometers to the north. To give our allies at The Unneeded Hypothesis all the answers they sought, I would have to find his remains.

Scobee expected a reply. "That's a corner I'm glad you didn't cut," I said.

"I've been haranguing them for flight plan approvals twice a day for the last week. We're still on schedule to evacuate, but that could slip if they delay us much longer and one of those field posts has more stuff left behind than we expect."

"I'll talk to the High Arbiter at ALECS local headquarters, and someone up in the ranks at USG. I was friends with Nesbitt Edmondson, and his wife Juliette, when I was first posted here. If he's still around—"

"He died."

"What?" I peered at him. Did he misspeak? Did I mishear? "I didn't know."

Scobee nodded his gaze down to his desktop. Death comes so unexpectedly these centuries. I read his avoidance of my gaze as a grant to me of privacy for grief and shock.

It also meant he saw no trace of a boyish longing shooting up the inside of my chest. *Her husband was dead, her other lover was dead, she might now turn to me—*

Scobee inhaled loudly enough for me to know he readied to speak. "It happened about five years ago. Some task in the wilds went wrong and he came back to the settlement in a body bag."

"If I see his wife, I'll give her my condolences." I forced my voice to sound casual. "Did she stay here after he died?"

"Last I heard. I can look her up for you."

"No need. She probably wouldn't remember me."

A knock on the open door turned my head. The woman looked to be in her twenties, hair thin and sandy-blond. She dressed like an office worker, in a white blouse and a pleated skirt hemmed just below her knee. A glance showed she lacked Juliette's depths.

She looked puzzled. "Are you *Daoshi* Lee?" She had an Australian accent, thick with earthy casualness, heightening the lack of depth.

"I am."

"Sorry, *Daoshi*, from your name, I was expecting you to be ethnically Chinese."

"I get that sometimes. You are?"

"Clio."

Scobee cleared his throat. "Clio will be on the final ship out. Her skills are too valuable to let her go before then."

To Clio, I said, "You do field work? Liase with ALECS local operations?"

"No, *Daoshi*. I'm in counterintelligence."

"We've been granted a flat for you," Scobee said, "on John Maynard Keynes Street a few blocks off Guru Nanak Boulevard. Clio will accompany you and get you situated."

"Thanks," I replied, then turned to her. "—but babysitting me seems a waste of your talents."

Clio held my gaze for a second. "*Daoshi*, I wish it were."

A few minutes later, my jitney drove from the depths of the garage and parked outside the double glass doors. It opened for us as we hurried into it. I let the vents blow cold air at my face for a few seconds before I turned to Clio. She held her finger in front of her lips and her eyes implored me. I nodded and she moved her finger away. "*Daoshi*, tell me news from Earth."

"You must get plenty of news already."

Muscles trembled in her neck. The jitney apparently picked up her subvocalization: the windows opaqued as if thick curtains had been drawn closed. For a moment, the cabin seemed dim, cool. She reached between two pleats of her skirt and pulled from some hidden pocket a case about ten centimeters long and three deep and high. A thumb-press flicked open a lid. Four rounded black balls, each smaller than the thumbnail of my little finger, lay in foam. "I've been too busy to follow it."

"You can't have left that long ago."

"I've been here two years. Please, *daoshi*, tell me news from Earth." She gave me a look urging me to comply.

"There's no news. Ninety-five percent of the human race takes their charitable allotment..."

Clio lifted a ball from the case. A half-ball, actually, its missing hemisphere previously hidden by the foam. She tapped its flat face and pressed it against a lower corner of the window on her side of the jitney. It clung to the window after she pulled her hand away.

I subvoked to her, "Are you worried about eavesdroppers?"

"I am," she replied the same way, her voice lilting through my earbuds. "But speak aloud."

I did as she asked. "...twenty kilograms of nanoassembled products and five hundred kilowatt-hours of fusion electricity every day—"

"Hasn't changed, then." She stuck another half-ball to the front window.

"A little. For the worse. Virtual reality games and immersive stories gain more popularity every day, and engagement with the real world drops in proportion. Except for our adherents, and those of the other ALECS spiritual communities, we're becoming a species bounded by nutshells and counting ourselves kings of infinite space."

Clio reached across me to press the next half-ball to the window on my side. Halfway there, her chest over my lap, she blushed and her eye visible to me widened. She left the seat to crouch on the floor, skirt covering more of her legs then I would have guessed possible, and I shifted my legs further from her. Her stare bored into the window where she pressed the half-ball. "You've talked enough for the system to calibrate your voice."

"Why does it need to do that?" I filled my voice with languid humor.

Once more on the seat next to me, she turned her back to press the last half-ball against the rear window. Between her shoulder blades, sweat formed a dark drop the size of a large antique coin. "The rattlers are an eavesdropping countermeasure."

"That implies an eavesdropping measure."

"Set off, please," she said to the jitney, aloud for my benefit. The jitney rolled forward. She crossed her legs, angling a knee toward me. Her face showed professional poise over traces of embarrassment. "When we speak, we create pressure waves in the air. When they hit a window, they set it to rattling. Not so much as we could notice, but aim a lidar—a laser rangefinder—on that window, and you could hear what we're saying."

What might USG security have heard during my ride from the spaceport? "The rattlers disrupt that."

"Yeah, but the two easiest rattler techniques give the game away. Easiest is a jitter pattern to feed the eavesdropper a white noise. That doesn't happen naturally. Next easiest is an interference pattern to cancel out our sound waves and feed the eavesdropper silence. But who ever is utterly silent for ten minutes in a jitney?"

"The rattlers are sending interference with an audio track."

"Exactly. Same principle as a noise-canceling earbud." Clio tapped her left ear. "We coded the system to improvise the audio track based on the jitney's passengers...." Her cheeks reddened. She turned away but forgot to subvocalize. Her inadvertent whisper came to me over the rush of air from the vents. "Is the system running a hook-up—?" Her cheeks grew even more red and a moment of alarm bulged her eyes.

Old habits stirred in me. I needled her embarrassment. "We wouldn't want that, would we?"

Her back stiffened and she half-turned away from me. I picked non-existent lint off my pants while the mood eased. I didn't have time for romantic encounters, especially not with the extra complications arising from crossing rank levels within a workplace.

And especially especially not if Juliette had no other man in her life.

We pulled up to a two-story walkup on John Maynard Keynes. "I'll double-check, but we've already secured your flat."

Flat like the flight deck of an archaic aircraft carrier. My new space was twice the size of my apartment on the downtown Calgary riverfront, and ten times the cramped apartment I'd shared with Appel-Ball during my first posting on Elard. The few pieces of furniture stood on spindly carbon nanotube legs and made the space even larger. Clio put her finger to her lips, then slid a device smaller than her palm from another hidden pocket of her skirt. She paced around, checking some visual data projected to her contact lenses, while the building's robots set down my luggage. After the robots left, she scanned my luggage, then blew out a breath. "I've spoofed their cameras and microphones, but I wager they'll try to plant more when you're out. I've set up intrusion sensors on the doors. Vibration detectors on the floor, in case they try to feed a device in from the flat below. You'll be free to speak here, in our headquarters, and in one of our jitneys. Anywhere else, assume you're being overheard."

"I will."

She nodded. "One last thing, *Daoshi*." She handed me the palm-sized device. I twirled it between my fingers. "That's yours till we leave. I'll do ongoing scans, but you're the first line of defense."

After Clio left, I rode my jitney down John Maynard Keynes to Guru Nanak Boulevard. I passed through the shadow of a tall building, taller than I remembered, at the corner. USG headquarters. The front facade showed only a bone-white brilliance dappled with reflective windows. I checked the upper floors for the joint of new growth, saw none. Impermeable to the eye, USG kept its secrets.

ALECS local operations stood half a kilometer further down Guru Nanak, at the intersection with Gregory Dialogus. Despite the addition to USG headquarters, ALECS local operations remained the tallest building on the planet. I waited on the top floor, where transparent interior walls combined with wide windows to give a view across dozens of kilometers, from far south out to sea to the lifeless gray mountains separating the plateau from the high desert to the north. Snow dusted the highest peaks like a dip in coarse salt.

Heavy footsteps sounded behind me, followed by a voice full of delight. "Darren! I knew you had come back, but I hadn't expected you to visit so quickly!"

I turned to Appel-Ball. He wrapped me in his burly arms and kissed my cheeks. "I didn't know I would have to," I said.

His jocular front faded. "Come to my office."

Appel-Ball's office occupied the southwest corner of the floor. From paintings hanging on the interior walls, English toffs from a bygone age judged us with their stares. The top of his wide, broad desk could sleep three and, knowing him, quite likely had.

I remembered Clio's warning about USG's eyes and ears. The

windows lacked rattlers. I sat facing his desk. My chair's leather squeaked and the nailhead trim was cool under my fingertips.

"You've come up in the world, High Arbiter."

His solemn moment in the lobby had disappeared. "As have you, old friend. A *daoshi* of the third rank? Almost high enough not to be sent interstellar on a pointless venture."

"I had the bad luck to have Elard on my resume."

"This planet is a curse upon us all." A drawer of his desk slid open and a telescoping arm extended a tray bearing two glasses and a bottle of Scotch. He affected an accent, badly. "A wee nip?"

I nodded. The cork thwoomed from the bottle. I sipped peaty amber liquid and said, "Curse or not, while I'm here, I will do Calgary some good. Our man Scobee tells me USG security forbids him access to some of our remote sites. You know that's a violation of ALECS protocols."

He shrugged. "What does that matter? You have some empty buildings in a desert no natives ever cross. There's no need to visit them. What, you think some native might stumble on them and happen to be literate enough in English to read the *Meditations* of Marcus Aurelius, the *Tao te Ching*, or those other titles—" He squinted, swatted the air with thick fingers. "—*Self-Therapy*, *The Trading Tribe*?"

I gave him a level look. "I have to make sure our remote sites are scrubbed, or we'll be in violation of ALECS protocols. We won't stoop to USG's level."

With a wry grin, he shook his head. "The West keeps getting in your way," he told me, for the hundredth time. He referred to all the archaic notions—the rule of law, respect for contract and custom, fair play, the rise and fall of individuals on merit rather than family connections or disparate impact regulations—that had propelled the human race a few thousand light years from Earth, then run out of fuel.

"You've become USG's tool, I see."

Ever the actor, he mugged a hurt look. "I still am the supreme human authority on this planet. But let us look at reality. I will strike ALECS' colors in a month. What would I gain by ruffling USG's feathers? Were I to tell them, 'you must abide by the rules,' they would just say, 'what is permitted to the gods is forbidden to oxen.' Not as eloquently, of course. Regardless, were I to repeat my demand, their agents would meet privately with the ALECS Executive Committee back on Earth, and I would be punished with an assignment even more inglorious than Elard."

"I understand the USG offices here are run by a newer arrival, named Vainqueur?"

"Don't bother." Appel-Ball gulped whisky.

"USG can't blow me off too much. If their agents try to meet privately with Calgary, the *daoshis* of the fourth rank would ignore them in retaliation."

Another wry head shake. "You are ever so naive. USG is strong and growing stronger, not just here and on other ALECS planets, but on Earth as well. You must know that better than I. They could make life difficult for The Way in the West by a thousand cuts."

Appel-Ball had it right. Parts of my subconscious shifted. "A shame Nesbitt died."

"You think were he still prominent with USG, he would pull strings to ensure his security personnel would give you passage?" His face softened. "Perhaps you are right. You two were part of a close circle, with Juliette and Purcell."

He stared at his Scotch for a time. Formerly he spoke frankly when in his cups, and rare is the man who grows out of that habit with age.

"What did you hear?" he asked. "About his death?"

"An accident, out in the wilds."

Appel-Ball sniffed out a breath. "Suicide."

I lifted my glass and held it front of my mouth. Nesbitt had been capable of many things, but suicide? "Why would he kill himself?"

"Because he could no longer take Juliette's ailment."

I frowned. Ailment? Any disease of the body could be treated. Likewise, any disease of the brain.

But a disease of the spirit... "What ailment?"

"She is a nymphomaniac."

My voice worked while the rest of me sat stunned. "The clinical term is 'sex addict.'" I took a swallow of Scotch. The whisky glowed down my throat. "You're serious."

"I had it from Baldassare. The official psychiatrist, recall him from our annual checkups?"

"Vaguely."

"He returned to Earth about ten years back. The night before he left, as the afterparty ran down, I pinned him in a corner and plied him with more drink. He was loose with many a person's secret, but hers was the only one that lodged in my mind. Juliette had all manner of affairs, and though she told him Nesbitt had no idea, Baldassare sensed from Nesbitt's checkups that he knew. Those hard edges, those steely eyes, Nesbitt repressed many emotions. Would you agree?"

What did Appel-Ball know about her affair with me? I blinked a few times. "I can't speculate."

"Her affairs dated back to your time on the planet. With hindsight, Baldassare realized Purcell had probably been one of her lovers. You did not notice?"

"No."

He leaned back, squinted. "I always assumed you were her emotional tampon. Someone she could use to satisfy her need to talk about her feelings, without caring about yours."

"'Dickless friend' would be pithier."

Appel-Ball spread wide his hands. "I've offended you. My pardons. We were all much younger and knew fewer of the ways of the world. I can tell you have grown as a man. When you meet her this visit, you will be free of the foolish hope she will open her heart and legs to you."

I angled my head in conciliation. "You were right about my relationship with her then. And what it would be if I met her now."

"But she never spoke of...?"

"The men she cheated on Nesbitt with? No. What woman in that situation would? Her words would stir up her male friend's jealousy. Either he would break off their friendship and take away her emotional tampon, or she would give him sexual sops out of guilt." Juliette, of course, had done the latter. Realizing that a few months after I left Elard had been one of the clearest moments of my life.

"You have indeed grown as a man." He raised his glass to me.

After I finished my Scotch, I rode back toward my flat. I could spend the rest of the long afternoon reviewing files from Scobee, and from the Unneeded Hypothesis, while Elar crawled toward the horizon. An early night, a fresh start in the morning—

A new message alert chimed in my ear. I subvoked, "Play."

Her voice, like old honey: sweet as ever, but gritted by time.

"Darren. Just the sound of your name takes me back to our younger days. You must meet me for dinner and catching up. The old café, twenty-five o'clock. The name has changed, but you recall the address. I'll get the table in the—in our—corner. Till then."

In my subconscious, my younger self jumped up at her command and ran to the old café. He thrashed within me while I sat immobile. The jitney continued down the scorched street. My younger self gave a confused, plaintive note and then sank back.

Presumptuous. Demanding. Flattering when it served her purpose. Juliette hadn't changed. But as Appel-Ball had put it, now I knew more of the ways of the world. She could wait in the café till closing, craning her long neck at each clang of the entry bell, while she found for herself what powerlessness felt like.

A wisdom from the Way passed through my awareness. If I avoided her to show I finally held some power over her, she still held power over me.

My thoughts ran more clearly. Her organization, the Universal Church of Christ, had long been in partnership with the United

Sodalities. She might be on good enough terms with her late husband's friends at USG to give Scobee's field teams the clearance they needed to scrub our remote sites.

And me clearance to find Purcell's remains.

I subvoked a reply message. "Till then."

After styling my hair and changing into slacks and a blazer, a few minutes before twenty-five, my jitney rolled along Gregory Dialogus. Elar lay two hours under the horizon. The lights of shops spilled out of transparent windows and pooled at the feet of strolling pedestrians. Jackets shielded the pedestrians against the cloudless desert night and the dregs of sea breeze that struggled up to the plateau. By day, I could have pretended the settlement kept its old crowds, and everyone lurked indoors until sunset. Not now. *Closed, please come again* slid and jumped around the opaque windows of half the shops. Most pedestrians had USG or UCC logos on their jacket sleeves. The transparent windows of restaurants and social clubs revealed unused tables and empty dance floors. Serving robots crouched at the doors like patient dogs.

My jitney took the parking spot immediately in front of the café. I climbed out and the artificial lights and the chill dry air dredged the sounds of talk, laughter, clanking plates, clinking glasses from the murk of memory. The structure remained unchanged, save for a scarred area of newer bone, roughly eighty centimeters wide by a meter twenty tall, to the right of the recessed doorway. In the past, the scarred area had held Greek letters in blue glass, forming an old poem, *The God Abandons Antony*. Now, float-mounted over the door, lighting strips formed Japanese characters in an icon of a wooden box.

The interior had been redone also, in red leather chairs and black lacquered tables. Near the door, three tables of USG and UCC personnel glanced up, eyes flat. A pale walking stick of a man came forward and bowed. "*Daoshi* Lee." His English had a Continental accent, and he comported himself in a manner more Japanese than a Japanese. We live in an age when the best sushi chefs are Dutch. "She arrived a few minutes ago. She said you would be able to guide yourself."

My mouth grew dry as I rounded the broad spur of bone shielding our usual corner from the USG and UCC personnel.

"Darren!" she said from an end of a bench, near a corner of the table.

One of the old writers had said, at fifty, a person has the face they deserve, and so much more true now. Age no longer leaves a mark. Only our social masks, and the emotions innervating our faces despite our wills, sculpt our expressions. Juliette remained beautiful, with brown hair now curling past her shoulders. But the decades had shaken her assurance. Something haunted her eyes. Perhaps Nesbitt's death—

—you finally feel guilt for all the men you toyed with?

I reseated my social mask. "A delight to see you." I leaned toward her and kissed her cheeks. Benches ringed the table on all sides. I'd always sat in a padded armchair to the right of where she sat now. My mind started down the trail of habit, but I resisted. I went to her left, on another bench, with a corner of the table between us.

She glanced down at the ebony point of the table corner, said nothing.

"I just heard about Nesbitt," I said. "My condolences."

"Thank you."

Drink orders. She took sake. The only draft beer was a lager from Park Slope. "Don't answer unless you want to, but how did it happen?"

She winced. "A cultural misunderstanding. He went out with a team of USG personnel and some natives representing the Indigenous Autonomous Council, to oversee humanitarian work at a distant village not yet fully acceded into the IAC. The bulls still trampled other bulls' offspring, other backward cultural practices like that. He said something wrong to a villager. No one around even heard what. But the villager took it wrong and fractured his skull before the other team members could intervene."

I studied her. She shrank away at first, but soon opened up, giving me a straighter look at her face and neck.

"You don't know what Appel-Ball says about it?"

"That old lecher? Of course you spoke to him, one has to call on the High Arbiter, that's the protocol. I always have admired your respect for protocol. Was he sad the sacred prostitutes of Ishtar shipped out two weeks back?"

I plowed through her chaff. "He says Nesbitt killed himself."

After a moment, she rolled her eyes. "You know you can't take everything he says at face value. Sometimes he puts the laser on the center of the target, other times he ablates a chunk of wall down-range. Nesbitt's death was the first sapient native attack in decades. It was an accident and we treated it as one."

"So Appel-Ball was wrong."

"Utterly. Nesbitt died in a good cause. Hard to believe it's been five years." Her hand crept across the table toward me.

I pulled my hand back, lifted my beer glass. "Did Nesbitt ever know about Purcell? Or me?"

Her shoulders stiffened. "Let's not talk about that."

"No? I left the planet because you let slip Nesbitt had hunted down Purcell out of jealousy and he'd do the same to me if her ever found out about my affair with you." I air-quoted. "'Let slip.' With Purcell gone missing, you were no longer torn between two lovers. You didn't need to unburden yourself to me anymore. With the choice between your husband and me, you chose your husband, and got rid of me by claiming to love me so much you wanted to see me safe on Earth."

My cramped apartment. Her plaintive look. *It's too dangerous for you to stay. I couldn't live with myself if you got hurt.* The memories ached, and the pain on her face failed to dull them. But the feelings pushed up by the memories washed away as part of me heard what I'd said. Why shouldn't she choose her husband? Why shouldn't she get her last surviving lover to depart? Before she'd lied to me in my cramped apartment, she'd known I would do as she told. If she'd spoken the truth, I would have stayed, and the three of us would have formed an unstable triangle that would eventually have shattered into fragments.

Juliette studied my face, then gathered herself with a breath. "You never spoke so harshly to me, before. I deserve it. I'm sorry. I should never have lied to you. After Purcell disappeared, my guilt about cheating on Nesbitt made me imagine he had killed him. I reached bottom. A moment of clarity—"

"We should never have been lovers." I softened my tone. "We were friends before that. Let's reconnect on those terms, if we can."

"Let's."

Dinner arrived in wooden boxes, styled like the icon above the front door. Inside, sliced bricks and logs of sushi rice encased tuna-flavored strips of uncooked protein and omega-3 fats. Fabricated in the settlement's nanoassembler within a few hours. D-chiral amino acids made up the native animals of the Elardian sea. They would taste rubbery and inflict diarrhea if eaten by terrestrial life.

I talked about my postings over the decades. Earth, Prawub, Olnosc. In the latter, as The Way in the West's director of local operations, I'd commissioned linguists to translate our recommended texts into three native languages. Then a promotion—

"So *daoshi* of the third rank is higher than it sounds." Juliette glanced at my left hand. "Are you—were you—married?"

"No. When lifespans are indefinite, there's always time later." I remembered my first stint back on Earth, late nights in the bars along the Calgary riverfront. My pose, aloofness masking a tortured Byronic soul. More women than I now cared to count had deluded themselves into bed with me. More times than I now cared to count, I'd exulted that seducing them punished their sex for having Juliette as a member.

From reading her face, I felt certain she sensed my thoughts.

She looked over my shoulder. Male banter came from behind me. Two USG men, one speaking in a tipsy, mentoring tone. "Remember, we don't want the natives to be more faithful to their customs. We don't want them to less faithful, either. We want them to be faithful to *our* customs."

Once they left earshot, I said, "Nice friends you have."

Propped up by her elbow, her hand unfurled like a blooming flower. "What's wrong with USG?"

"What's wrong?" I scowled at her. "As a member of their sister organization, you might not see it. They encroach on the rest of us every chance they get. Today they scrutinized me at the spaceport and on my way into town, in violation of ALECS protocols. Worse, they've denied Scobee access to some of our old field sites—"

"They have? Where?"

"Half a dozen places off to the north."

"That explains it." She paused while the two men walked past us back toward their table. "USG and UCC have ongoing missionary work among the native tribes along the coast where the sea curves around to the north. The Indigenous Autonomous Council wants to minimize the risk of further missionary work by disapproved spiritual communities. No offense."

"I'd take none, if the natives actually chose that and their human allies simply relayed the message. Yet how are the rest of us to know?"

Juliette angled her head and lifted her chin, exposing more of her neck. "If they scrutinize you so much, should you be talking about such things?" Her voice sounded playful, but for a moment, her tone did not match a tightening of the fine muscles around her eyes.

I drew in a breath and held my mouth open to imbue my next words with a meaning some electronic eavesdropper would not pick up. "It's been a long day of travel and meetings, and my frustration with the denied access to our field sites is spilling out. Of course USG earned approval from a quorum of native polities. Of course the natives want the rest of us gone. I feel frustrated because we're trying to do that. If the natives want a full cultural decontamination, we have to go out to our old sites, pry up the metaphorical floorboards, and if we find any of our recommended texts we left behind, toss them in the nanoassemblery's recycling bin."

"I understand your frustration."

Another glass of beer arrived. I hadn't noticed my first one disappear. Time to slow down. "That's all you can do?"

"What do you mean?"

I quirked an eyebrow. "You've been on Elard longer than anyone else, except possibly Appel-Ball. Your organization is the only one staying here with USG after the rest of us head back to Earth. I suspect your rank is higher than you're letting on."

She leaned back and hugged herself across her upper abdomen. "You want me to push USG to give you access to those field sites."

"Friends do one another favors. We are friends, right?"

"Are we? Do friends ask friends to push against the new order of the world?"

I mimicked her earlier tone. "If they order your world so much, should you be talking of such things?"

She fixed me a look I'd never before seen her give me. Notes of admiration, respect, even a little fear, all leaking out from her brown eyes. I gazed back, unblinking, until she spoke.

"It will take a few days. Be patient. I'll contact you."

I expected the next few days to drag by, and at first they did. Every morning promptly at ten o'clock, Scobee briefed me on the previous day's results and the new day's plans. He anticipated my questions about the day's plans and always reported completion of the work of the previous. His right eye drooped more and the bags under his eyes grew thicker and more purple. When I left my large, nearly empty guest office at twenty o'clock, he might hold his head low over data on his desk, or his voice on a call to some subordinate might spill impatience out his door.

From the polarized southerly windows of my guest office, Elard crawled up and down the sky. I could do nothing to help The Way in the West shut down its operations. Perhaps I could help the Unneeded Hypothesis find answers about Purcell's disappearance.

I reviewed the files given to me in Prague, for the dozenth time. In the last months before his disappearance, Purcell reported multiple field trips to native villages near the north coast. As it happened, not far from the sites USG kept us from visiting. Purcell's final flight plan repeated a journey to a village he knew, but for some reason, he veered off course near some badlands about two hundred kilometers to the northwest of our settlement. Traffic control lost sight of him a few minutes later. Rescue teams soon found his empty airmobile, then traversed hundreds of square kilometers of jumbled terrain for three weeks, until simulations indicated he would have run out of water and food.

Trained rescuers hadn't found him, and my odds were even worse than theirs. I checked and double-checked the files, looking for something to track him from the abandoned airmobile. On my own, I found nothing.

Scobee inadvertently gave me the answer I needed. In his office one morning, my gaze ran down the day's to-do list, overlaid by our augmented reality contact lenses on our views of the wall near his door. "This is a lot."

"We'll get it done." He sounded tired. "Just like we got a lot done yesterday, and the day before."

My gaze stopped at an entry. *Review physical effects at ALECS lost & found.* I pointed at the task. "I'll take this one. Your team saves a person-day looking through boxes in a warehouse, and I don't sit in an office playing solitaire."

Scobee grunted. "Knock yourself out."

ALECS Unclaimed Property occupied a warehouse on the east side of the settlement. Near the front corner of the building, a single door faced a shaded parking lot. An awning stretched from the building to poles on the far side. I climbed out of my jitney. The mid-morning air baked me and the awning's fabric rippled in a faint breeze.

Inside, my eyes adjusted to a dim, shabby room. Years of use had scuffed the gypsum board walling the room off from the bulk of the warehouse. The leatherette of chair-arms in the waiting area had cracked, and a strip of unglued veneer dangled outward from the edge of a table.

In the far corner, a chair creaked. A throat cleared. "May I help you?" A male voice, labored with breaths.

"I'm Darren Lee, with The Way in the West. I'm here on behalf of our operations-suspension team, to review any physical effects of ours you might have in custody."

The man stayed in his chair. He looked as if his body had molded itself around it. "Have a seat, *Daoshi* Lee, and I'll see what we have of yours." He subvoked a few commands, then shut his eyes. "You just come out from Earth?"

"I did."

"I'm Olivenberg. Is there something important of yours in the warehouse?"

"Important?"

"Your bosses sent you here from Earth to look at unclaimed property?"

I chuckled, then shook my head in the manner of exasperated employees. "I'd be astonished if there's anything of interest to anyone in your warehouse, but you tell that to my headquarters."

"They want to keep their laundry lists out of USG's hands. Can't blame them. USG thinks a fingerprint from a blank chip could be an exploit." He shut his eyes again. "You've got six boxes."

"How are they labeled?"

"Organization, last known individual's name, location where found, date logged in. They'll be filed under W. If you still can't find them, message me."

"I can't just wave for the cameras?"

"We don't have any inside the warehouse."

I raised an eyebrow. "*You* don't."

"The changeover hasn't happened yet."

I nodded. "Will you stay on?"

"And work for USG? I'm heading back to Earth. Twenty years

was long enough. Time to claim the matter and energy minimum while I figure out what to do next."

Sounded like he already claimed a minimum lifestyle. But like any bureaucrat, he succored himself with self-delusions of his job's importance. "Thanks for all you've done. You're a credit to ALECS."

He shrugged and gestured over his shoulder at a door into the warehouse. "I leave at twenty o'clock. Be back here five minutes before."

My footsteps echoed through the warehouse. Huge lighting strips wandered across the ceiling. At the warehouse's far end, daylight, dust, and heat leaked around the roll-up door of a loading dock. A breeze rattled the door against its track. Shelves bolted to the floor held plastic boxes, and larger crates stood on racks mounted to the straight, lower reaches of the walls. The space smelled of aged plastic, and d-handed native biomolecules borne in by the wind.

A set of long tables, beige tops on flimsy-looking, but sturdy, carbon nanotube legs, filled a central clearing. I nudged a chair with my foot to claim a table, then set off for shelves labeled *W-Z*.

A robotic cart whispered to a stop near me as I found the first of our boxes. "Would you like some assistance, sir?"

I yanked the box out and held it against my hip. Clio's admonitions trumped my middling confidence in Olivenberg's words. "I'll walk with it. And a few others. Every little way to maintain muscle mass helps," I added, for the sake of any USG security personnel who might be listening through it.

"As you wish, sir. If you change your mind, I'll be at the recharging station in the southeast corner." It rolled away.

I carried the box to the table, then went after the next. I repeated the process for the remaining three boxes. The five formed a pyramid on the table.

Five? Olivenberg's database lookup had returned six.

I returned to the shelf. Not there. Not behind a solitary box owned by Zoroastrian Revival. Where, then, was the sixth box for Way in the West, The?

The question gave me its own answer. I checked the signs on the ends of each shelving unit, looking for *T*, then found it. My path took me past *U*. I slowed my steps and glanced at the shelves for *Unneeded Hypothesis, The*. None there.

I took my next steps even faster than before.

A box stood on a lower shelf. I knelt and pulled it toward me. *The Way in the West*, its label read. Behind it stood another box. The only sides I could see were blank. I tugged and turned it.

Organization: The Unneeded Hypothesis
Last known owner: Purcell, Ward

My heart thudded. I pulled the box out and stacked it on the other one. I grasped the long sides of the lower box to keep Purcell's name hidden against my chest, then carried them both to my table.

After setting them down, and rearranging them to hide Purcell's name, I returned my mind to my official task. Yet all morning, while I sifted through the forgotten belongings of my fellow *daoshis* and acolytes, my mind wandered to Purcell's box. At the old café, he often sat back with an archaic sketchbook, its pressboard cover flipped onto his knee, and scratched a pencil over nanoassembled paper, with occasional pauses to say something caustic to the rest of us.

Finally, after I filled a recycling bag with unwashed coffee cups, cracked flying discs, a bag of sand accompanying a desktop zen garden, and other leftovers of my distant colleagues' lives, and collected our few data chips for secure destruction at our offices, I opened Purcell's box. Stacks of sketchbooks greeted me.

I'd only ever glimpsed his drawings at steep angles, in passing. Seeing them straight-on, with time to study them, amazed me. Lines and shadings of graphite did more than represent us as we had been. They revealed aspects of us I had never before so clearly noticed. A manipulative streak tightening the skin between Juliette's eyebrows and upper lids. Nesbitt's flat look of loaded, cocked criticism needing only a squeeze of the trigger to fire. My callowness slackening my cheeks. I had not seen that look since the shaving mirror in my old, tiny quarters. If I'd even seen it then.

I flipped through more sketchbooks. Each drawing showed in the lower right corner a date and a location, in block letters whose strokes never quite touched, as well as a scrawl of his surname. Each sketchbook as a whole focused on a single topic. The three of us in the old café—Juliette, nude under rumpled sheets in Purcell's apartment—from field work, closeups of natives showing emotions I could not read.

In the latter, he came to focus on one individual. A bull, with a scar down one of its cooling crests and a thousand-yard stare in its hawed eyes. After a dozen pages of this bull came the torn stub of a page ripped out.

Sketchbook after sketchbook, page after page, I flipped. The specificity of each sketchbook to a topic meant often the latter pages showed only creamy white, virginal and dead. I flipped anyway, in case he had some secret purpose. While going through blank pages in a sketchbook of buildings around the settlement, the last date about eight months before his disappearance, my fingertip found an edge folded over by a couple of millimeters.

The next page had nothing to do with ALECS architecture. It showed a map. The settlement, the slender curving sea, the mountain ranges and types of desert stretching from our location a thousand kilometers to the north. The margins held cryptic notes—"the red canyon," "the bull leaning on the cow," others even more obscure. Squares with curt abbreviations depicted Unneeded Hypothesis field sites, I surmised.

Circles dotted the map, scores of kilometers from any other habitation, human or native. Around the circles, latitude and longitude coordinates. Xs marked some of the circles, with dates overlapping that of this book's last sketch. The latest X's date was two weeks before his disappearance. The circles and Xs bore no pattern that I could see.

I recalled the files Purcell's colleagues had given me, and matched their maps to this one. Purcell's final flight had landed about eight kilometers from an unmarked circle.

I hid the sketchbook under the packet of data chips to be securely destroyed back at local operations. Most of the boxes, now empty, I broke down and tossed into the recycling bag. The two sorted by *The* I took back to their shelf of origin.

I knew where to go. If I could leave the settlement.

The possibility of being trapped in the settlement soured my mood for the rest of the day. I went to the fitness club and tried to fight off the mood by attacking a kettlebell routine, more sets of more reps than usual of swings and get-ups. Sweat left a salty rime under the arms and on the lower back of my wicking shirt. Heart knocking, I kept going, twenty-four kilos, another fifty swings—

"Darren?"

I managed to safely settle the kettlebell on the mat between my feet. "Juliette, what's?" I toweled sweat off my face and caught my breath.

"Pilates class." She dressed the part, black spandex clinging to her legs and torso, hair pulled back to cast her cheekbones in sharper relief. Her gaze slid over my upper arms and chest. "I was going to call from my jitney, but when your software assistant showed you were here, I decided to tell you in person. I explained your situation to Vainqueur and he cleared your people to revisit your last four abandoned sites."

"Thanks." I had more breath now. "I'd offer to do you a favor in return, but we both know there's nothing I can do for you."

She drew a breath. "Don't be so sure."

I peered at her. Did she still have some hope of rekindling our long-gone tryst? I gave an exaggerated look down and to the right, to let her know I checked the time in the corner of my augmented reality display. "Don't miss your class on my account."

"Okay. One last thing. Would you have time to meet again before you leave?"

"Probably. Just one condition: no sushi." I nodded to her, then reached for the kettlebell.

I went out the day after with our first field team, to the surprise of its leader, a narrow-chinned man named Kapodistrias. As our van waited at the entry gate for the airfield, Kapodistrias asked me questions about how the team should work and nodded at my responses. Once we were airborne, he gave the team instructions he had already planned. I spent the next hour staring out a window at the jumbles of sand and rock, dune and scarp, defining the high desert north of the settlement.

What had Purcell looked for out here?

Had Juliette's long-ago hint, that Nesbitt had killed Purcell, been true? Out of jealousy? Or did it relate to something else?

We landed. Before Kapodistrias raised the airmobile's rear hatch, we donned and double-checked our polarized face shields, air-conditioned cloaks, water packs, drinking tubes, and sunblock lotion on the backs of our hands. Over the protests of some acolytes, I slung a portable air conditioner over my shoulder as the hatch lifted.

Outside, the day seemed brighter, hotter, dryer than it ever did in the ALECS settlement. The exhaust fans mounted on the others' backs poured out streams of broiling air. We walked in line, not column, to the old site.

Up a slope, three structures hunkered, half-burrowed into the rocky soil. Double layers of thick plastic covered each structure's windows and doors. A reprogrammable sign still held our logo and the name of the station, but the pigment molecules, long fixed in position, had faded in decades of sunlight. Beyond the station, the granite peaks of the last mountain range before the sea jutted into the pallid blue sky.

Team members parted the double layer of plastic covering the main building. Radio chatter called for the portable air conditioner and I hustled up. They opened the building's front door before I got there. Slightly cooler air, thick and stale, slithered under my face shield. One person aimed the air conditioner down an interior hallway, while another routed its vent out the part in the plastic, and a third sprayed temporary solar cells on the building's roof. Soon the inside had cooled enough for us to turn off the cooling function of our cloaks.

The main building held offices and a store'n'cook kitchen on one side of the interior hallway, and a meeting space on the other. Same layout as other field sites, where I'd led spiritual retreats with The Way in the West personnel and a few natives, bachelor bulls all. The chairs and couches in the meeting space formed a circle, as if the site had been abandoned in the middle of a retreat. Team members surveyed the room, looking for forgotten data, especially any eye-readable text. My interface projected deepening shades of green over my view of the meeting space as the probability forgotten data eluded us dropped toward zero.

The smaller buildings, accessible through shaded tunnels lit by thin, near-opaque windows near the ceilings, held sleeping and recreation quarters. The air conditioner could not reach so far, but Kapodistrias had ordered the team to keep their cooling units turned off. Sweat stung my eyes and ran down my neck as the team searched. The departed personnel had been sloppy. Data chips with broken cases lay forgotten under unmade beds.

"Remember," Kapodistrias announced over the team's radio net, "if it looks like it might be proprietary, bag it for local ops and—brambles in the path."

I shared a puzzled look with the other team members in the room.

Kapodistrias spoke, more urgently. "*Daoshi* Lee, please join me at the front entrance. Quickly, if you please."

I found him just outside the front door. The roar of the air conditioner's exhaust fan echoed off the plastic. Outside, partially clouded by the plastic, a trio of airmobiles had landed near ours, and armed humans in desert camouflage waited in line.

"I thought you'd cleared us, *Daoshi*."

"You're not the only one. Let's greet our guests." I turned on the cooling unit in my cloak, spread my fingers wide, and went out the parting in the plastic, palms-first.

Once clear of the plastic, I spread my arms wide, like Jesus—no, that was not a name to conjure USG with. Certainly USG had its martyrs, but I did not know their names. I took three steps, squinting despite my face shield. Kapodistrias' footsteps crunched the rocky soil behind me.

"Stop there," boomed an amplified voice from the figure in the center of the line. "Identify yourselves."

"Darren Lee, *daoshi* of the third rank, of The Way in the West. I have a dozen colleagues with me, ten inside, two staying with our airmobile."

"What are you doing here?"

"Complying with ALECS protocols by eliminating ideological or spiritual data from our facilities, prior to withdrawal from Elard. We're unarmed. I'm going to lower my hands now."

Behind my shoulder, Kapodistrias muttered, "*Daoshi—*"

I dropped my hands to my sides. The USG security personnel shifted their weight and glanced toward their spokesman. For a moment, confusion showed across his shoulders. Finally, he set his hands on his hips and jutted his chest toward us. "As a gesture of goodwill, we'll take your word for it, for now."

Security personnel? Was not my spiritual community dedicated to seeing the universe as it was?

I stared at a line of soldiers.

Their spokesman—squad leader, I corrected myself—said, "Are you aware the Indigenous Autonomous Council has decreed this region is to be free of unauthorized human activity?"

"So I've heard. Are you aware we have to scrub any record of our beliefs from all our sites?"

The squad leader shrugged. "How you put a round peg in a square hole is not my problem."

"Vainqueur granted us permission. I mean, the IAC granted us permission, and Vainqueur relayed that news to us."

A wave of agitated body language rippled through the line of soldiers. The squad leader swayed away from me and shifted a foot backward to plant his weight. "Vainqueur."

"Yes. Did I mispronounce his name?"

"Relayed that news to you."

"Not directly, but I have his authorization from someone who has his... ear."

The squad leader stepped forward. "Be that as it may, Mr. Lee, at first glance, you and your subordinates are in violation of an IAC decree. You and your subordinates are hereby directed to return to your airmobile, pending investigation of your claim. If you truly have IAC permission, you'll be allowed to resume decommissioning this site. If not, we'll escort you back to the settlement, and any of you found leaving the perimeter again will be locked in the brig until the last ship lifts off."

Kapodistrias grunted.

"Throw away the bitter cucumber," I told him, "and get the team back in the airmobile." To the USG soldiers, I said, "We'll wait in our vehicle."

Sealed up in the airmobile, many of my team members grumbled about the delay. One young man, red-haired and ruddy-cheeked, even asked me, "Do we really have clearance? Or do you think you can waltz in from Earth and bluff those thugs?"

The conversations around us froze.

"I don't," I said. "We do." I stared at the redhead until he blinked and turned away.

Time passed, until an armored glove rapped on the rear hatch. Our cooling units roared to life as Kapodistrias opened up.

The squad leader stood with hands on hips, and a glum set to his shoulders. He craned his neck and searched through the crowd for me. "Your authorization is confirmed, *Daoshi* Lee. My apologies for the delay. If my team can assist you, here or at another site—"

"We welcome your offer, but there's no need. Good day."

The squad leader trudged away while my team lifted its equipment to return to the site. I reached for the portable air conditioner, but the redhead lunged past me, then hoisted the unit to his shoulder. We returned to the site in high spirits, which remained with us as we finished our work. Twilight darkened the sky as we flew back to the settlement. I pulled a flask from my pack and handed it around.

When we landed, I boarded the same van as Kapodistrias, and took a seat next to him. "You should have no problems on your future missions. You won't need me to accompany you. But I reserve the right to fly out on my own and snap inspect your team."

The next morning, after meeting with Scobee, I went to my office. A few minutes to write a brief report on the previous day's actions, then hours to spend studying Purcell's map—

"*Daoshi* Lee," said the building, "you have a guest in the lobby."

"A guest?"

The building sent a camera image to my contact lenses. Juliette, her eyebrows crinkled, mouth tight.

"What does she want?"

"She would not tell me," the building said.

I closed Purcell's sketchbook, slid it in a drawer. "Let her in."

"I will relay your authorization to Clio. Scobee has ordered that she accompany any guests at all times in the building."

"Sounds like I'll see them both." I locked the drawer with my thumbprint and waited for them to come.

Clio's accent heralded her approach. "...We're truly honored *Daoshi* Lee came out from Earth to help us decommission our facilities. I've learned a lot from him."

Juliette paused a moment. "I'm sure you have."

They halted in the doorway. Clio knocked. "*Daoshi?* Is now a good time?"

"As good as any. Come in." From my seat, I waved across the desk, at two chairs. "Sit, please."

Juliette paused halfway between standing and sitting. She lifted an eyebrow at Clio. "My business is with *Daoshi* Lee."

"Since I'm his assistant, I ought to sit in."

Seated, Juliette said, "My conversation with your boss is private."

I cleared my throat. "Clio is the soul of discretion."

Juliette turned to me a cautious gaze. "You can tell her to take ten minutes."

"I can. But I won't. What brings you by, in person?"

She crossed her legs and enmeshed her fingers into a double fist of prayer on her lap. "I heard about your difficulty yesterday with a USG security flunky. I want to apologize."

"Apologize? We suffered a two-hour delay. An inconvenience, nothing more."

"You shouldn't have had to suffer even that." She pressed her lips together before speaking her next words. "I spoke to Vainqueur and he promised you would be cleared to visit your old sites."

"You did all I asked of you. On top of that, he honored your promise. I seek no apology." I narrowed my eyes. "You expected him to tell everyone in USG security to stay out of our way? That's a high expectation to pile on yourself."

Juliette stretched her neck. "I rank highly in UCC's local operations. My requests to USG are always honored to the full."

She remained lovely, despite having a vulnerability to her now that I had not seen in our past. I shoved the thought away. "Clearly not *always*," I told her. "Yesterday, Vainqueur didn't tell everyone about his approval of our trip. Maybe he didn't see the need to honor your request to the full by relaying it to all his subordinates. Or perhaps he did, but his subordinates dithered about informing all of their underlings. Or, simply, it's a bureaucracy, and the left-hand official doesn't know what the right-hand one is doing."

"None of those are acceptable excuses—"

"What bothers you about this? You thought you had more influence over USG's local operations? You don't. You did once? We've all gotten older, and the worlds have changed out from under us. Thank you again for putting in a word with Vainqueur, and my team and I are walking around the settlement today instead of cooling our heels in the brig, so your word to Vainqueur was enough. Is there anything more? I have the rest of my day's work to get to."

Her eyes widened before a social mask returned to her features.

"You're busy. I understand." She glanced sidelong at Clio, then stiffened her shoulders to exclude the other woman from our conversation. "Maybe we can meet some evening. The sushi place?"

"I hated the ambiance."

"A café, a bar?"

Had I ever sounded so needy, asking her for trysts? *Now she knows how I felt* and the thought's pettiness shamed me. "I'll check my schedule. Take care."

Clio led Juliette from the room. Juliette, vulnerable and confused. None of us would have imagined it, during my first tour on Elard. She had known the rules of the world, and how to apply them to her benefit. But the rules had since changed, and her skill at applying them had ossified.

My petty thoughts returned. She was mortal, after all. Yet those petty thoughts brought with them sympathy. She was human, and capable of making a mutual connection. That capability had been beneath the Juliette of decades ago.

Even so, it didn't matter. I had a duty to The Way in the West that trumped any wish to try reconnecting with her.

The next few days I worked in the office, except for one snap inspection of the field team. One hour airborne each way, with no one to talk to but the autopilot. As expected, all was in order, but any USG spies watching me would now think nothing of me flying alone into the desert. Late each afternoon, I talked with Kapodistrias to find his plans for the next day, then hurried back to my office to match the flight path I would be expected to take on a "snap inspection" against the circle on Purcell's map nearest his point of disappearance.

The evening of the second day before our withdrawal, I found they were bound for their final site, two hundred kilometers past the site of Purcell's disappearance. I checked the time. A few minutes after twenty o'clock. On my way down the elevator to my jitney, I sent a message to Appel-Ball. "Do you have time to meet?"

He called as the jitney rolled toward my flat. My augmented reality engine projected his image onto my contact lenses so that he seemed to sit on the rear-facing seats across the jitney's cabin. "I'm not in the office."

"I guessed. I have an unofficial purpose. A few minutes over drinks. I wouldn't be keeping you from anything?"

"No. Other than your blonde Aussie-ette, almost all the ladies have gone. I'm at the Anfield, on Guru Nanak Boulevard, across and half a block down from ALECS headquarters."

I parked in a mostly empty multi-level garage shared by a number of shops. After a short walk through turbulence flung by fans taller than me, I entered the pub. Dim lights, cool air, walls decked with pennants of European soccer clubs. No sound but the antique audio-video displays chattering with British-accented play-by-play of a match played on Earth two months ago.

While the bartender drew for me a glass of stout, I asked, "You're staying?"

He had some flavor of British accent. "Them USG blokes need a place to raise a pint, yeah? Besides, they like football. I see their five-year-old kids on the covered field near the primary school, running through drills." He set my glass on the bar. Its head was as stiff as a crystallized cloud. "Your mates are at a back table. Can't miss them."

Deeper in the pub, Appel-Ball sat at the head of a table with three younger-looking ALECS men along the sides. Shouts of displeasure erupted from all four of them. The monitors replayed a shot glancing off the outside of a goalpost. "How could he miss that?" Appel-Ball said, then noticed me. He waggled a finger at me. "I don't want to hear that Marcus Aurelius bit from you."

"If I told it to you, I'd be asking, 'why were such things made in the world?'"

He frowned and bobbed his head from side to side, then shook his head with a wry smile. "You think too much, old friend. Sit, drink."

The first half ticked by. Appel-Ball and his colleagues cheered and booed the action while I sipped my beer. Soccer is like hockey, but slower, and with prima donnas.

When the referee's whistle announced halftime, I said, "I'll take those few minutes now." I aimed a hitchhiker's thumb at an interior corner, far from the windows.

His eyebrow flexed upward, but he pushed back his chair and went with me. He leaned his elbow on a high table. "What do you need, Darren?"

"Do you still run air traffic control? Or has USG already taken charge?"

"The crew is still all ALECS."

I mirrored his posture, elbow on table. "I'll be flying out tomorrow, around twelve or thirteen o'clock. Once I'm a hundred kilometers north, I want air traffic control to log me as following my flight plan."

"Where will you be going that the rest of us cannot know?"

"I want a few last hours alone on Elard. In the wilds, total solitude, just me and my thoughts."

"You could have that while following a flight plan."

I looked him straight in the eye. "I'd rather not."

He chuckled, a single exhalation broken into a series of sniffs. "You are a poor liar, Darren. Relax. It makes me no mind why you want this. And we are old friends, so I'm inclined to grant this. But since this matters so much to you, I would disserve ALECS if I gave it to you without getting something in return."

"I'm sure we can come to an arrangement."

He wetted his lips. "I will be on the same outbound ship as you and the blond Aussie-ette. Her name again?"

I stood tall and folded my arms over my chest. "I wouldn't pimp her out, even if I could, which I cannot."

He chuckled again. "Of course. If you haven't already pierced her defenses, you have your own plan to do so on the trip to Earth. You need only have told me."

"She's a fraction of my age. Yours too."

Appel-Ball shook his head. "You are a gentleman from a golden age, sent by accident into our age of brass. What then can you offer me?"

From the displays, the announcers recapped the first half's highlights.

"The last few weeks, I looked into how you came to be high arbiter. By default. No one wanted to come from Earth to be a caretaker of the inevitable handover to USG. So you received a promotion you would not have gotten anywhere else."

"If you're attempting to flatter me—"

"I'm telling you about the universe as it is."

"Rare is the man who wants to hear *that*."

I went on. "And you already know the truth of what I say."

"The man who wants such a thing dragged into daylight is rarer still. But go on."

"Returning to Earth means a demotion for you. Either an office job in ALECS headquarters or a minor role in an interstellar mission. Your best chance of a position more suitable for your present status is to cultivate an ally. Do this and I'll make sure The Way in the West puts its thumb on the scale for you in meetings of the ALECS personnel committee."

A display over his shoulder showed teams returning to the pitch. Appel-Ball scraped his fingers over his smooth cheeks. "What guarantees can you offer?"

"Beyond my reputation, and The Way in the West's? None, but what can you offer me?"

He chuckled again. "You have a deal. Before I return to the match, one thing. Would that thumb on the scale be denied me if I attempted to charm the blonde Aussie-ette on the flight to Earth?"

"She can make her own decisions." Especially if I soured her on Appel-Ball.

"Betimes your West shows you your way. You shall have what you ask."

"We'll remember your willingness to work with us. Enjoy the second half." I clapped my hand on his shoulder and left.

The next morning, I went to the airfield at ten-thirty. The USG security men at the settlement exit and the entrance to the airfield asked me my name and organization, then waved me through. Their impending triumph made them lazy.

At the operations hut, the clerk fed my interface the hangar location of my airmobile for the day. A sleek gray runabout. Years of desert travel had abraded the ALECS logo on its side. I palmed Clio's scanner and walked around the vehicle.

USG security had glued a tracker inside the cargo bin. Clio's scanner had a sharp enough edge for me to pry it off. I dropped it to the hangar floor and crunched it under my boot heel, then climbed in and took off.

Thirty minutes later, a thousand meters up, my airmobile slowly circled the coordinates of one of the circles on Purcell's map. The terrain rose and fell. Hills partially masked lower ground behind them. Salt pans glared at Elar. A few large boulders lay about.

Aha. What appeared to be one large boulder, when seen from a good angle, was really two. A pillar of rock had slumped down on a rounder one.

A bull leaning on a cow.

Just beyond them, a fold in the terrain turned out to be a narrow canyon. Its floor was red as dried human blood.

Two runs along the red canyon showed it to be banana-shaped, about eight hundred meters long and a hundred-fifty wide. A scarp formed its south face, and a steep but walkable slope, its north. The top of the north slope merged into rolling terrain climbing up to a line of hills about two kilometers away. No sign of human or native activity.

I told my airmobile to land in the canyon. The engines' roar echoed off the scarp. I touched down on the canyon floor, about three hundred meters from the rock formation and a hundred meters from the scarp. The engines cut out.

An irregular pattern of jagged holes showed along a section of the scarp wall. They could have passed as natural, save for several elongated holes reaching down to the depression floor. Most were the size of a standing human or native. One would allow an airmobile to enter, or two off-road jitneys abreast.

I donned my water bottle, cooling cloak, face shield. I subvoked to the cameras in my contact lenses and the microphones in my earbud to *record*, checked the time- and location-stamps were on, and went out.

The cooling fans in my cloak whirred at full speed as I set out into the hot midday air. Despite the insulation in my boot soles, I hopped from foot to foot across the red canyon floor. The shade along the foot of the scarp cooled my footing, but the cooling fans remained at full speed.

I went in the largest hole. My guess of jitneys seemed even more right. Through a layer of dust on the floor showed the white lines of empty parking spaces. I walked on.

Deeper in, large, empty rooms. Holes in floors and ceilings suggested bolts holding long-gone furniture. The dimensions of the bolt holes could have meant bunks, kitchens, dining halls, storerooms, tall upright racks like the ones holding cues in the poolhalls down by the downtown Calgary riverfront.... Dozens of sapients, and their equipment, could have dwelled here at a time.

Outside, I stood in the shade and looked around. High above, an airmobile flew to the north. I double-took and peered at it. Its line of flight continued on, seemingly oblivious to my airmobile parked on the red canyon floor.

I let out a breath. What I sought would be at ground level. There, on the depression's slanted north slope, a couple hundred meters away, was that...? I trudged through the heat. The cooling fan's whine became a roar.

I sucked water through a straw as I studied the item. A line of eight bone-white plugs, each as thick as my forearm, extended about ten centimeters above the ground. Decades of wear had rounded each plug's edge. I stooped for a closer look and a drop of sweat stung my eye.

From the center of each plug's top surface rose a few millimeters of metal showing the smooth cut of a laser saw.

Behind the line of plugs, a long, narrow mound of brown and tawny rocks, gravel, and pebbles ran parallel to the line of plugs. Too straight, and too different from the red rock of the canyon floor, to be natural. A firm touch on the mounded particles told me the mound had greater cohesion than a first glance would have guessed. Spray-on adhesive? My gloved fingers traced the smooth surface of the adhesive coating the outside of the mounded rocks—wait—

Something had spalled chunks the size of a baby's fist from large rocks, and torn pockets about the same size from regions of the mound formed from gravel and pebbles. The spalled and torn regions occurred in vertical lines, each line about as far from its neighbors as the plugs in the canyon floor were from each other.

From one damaged area in the mound, I drew a line in my mind's eye through the nearest plug, and extended it across the canyon floor. About a hundred meters away, another line of eight bone-white plugs jutted just above the ground. Nearby, an L-shape of more bone suggested the foundation of a building.

I did not know where Purcell's body lay, but I had a strong inkling why he had died.

From the mound, I hiked up the canyon's northern slope. Loose particles slid under my boots and skittered downslope. The northern rim of the canyon gave good views of both the dwelling dug out of the scarp and the line of plugs in front of the mound. Near the canyon rim sat a large boulder, roughly teardrop-shaped. Slivers of daylight showed under the boulder's sides, where shallow depressions looked scooped out by decades of wind.

I went around the boulder, then stopped. My breaths roared inside my face shield.

Behind the boulder, another shallow depression marred the ground. What stopped me were its contents.

Half-buried by wind-blown dirt, a corpse lay face up. I did not know for certain it was Purcell, but of *corpse* I lacked all doubt.

I knelt next to the dead man. My face grew clammy.

Purcell. His face shield had been pushed up, exposing his desiccated features. His lips had pulled back from a mouth locked in his dying agony. Narrow, shallow slits went through the flesh of his ears on both sides of the canals, and two more had opened his eyeballs to the elements. I looked for earbuds and the thin clear discs of augmented reality contact lenses, but failed to find them.

The front of his cloak hung loose, its seam sliced by a sharp knife. I flicked the fabric panels aside. His shirt had been shredded to reveal his thin chest, tufted with a few hairs over his breastbone. Thick flaps of skin had been cut open in the upper right and left of his chest, about five centimeters below each collarbone. I tightened my mouth and poked a finger under each flap. The processors and local storage for Purcell's augmented reality hardware had been cut out, and with them, any data stored in it after being copied from the cameras in his missing contact lenses.

What did you see? His killer had wanted to ensure, even in death, Purcell could not answer my question.

How had he died? The knife wounds looked too shallow to be fatal, and the front of his body lacked other signs of violence. I moved next to his torso and pushed up. With little effort, his dried-out body rolled onto its side.

A laser rifle fired from a shallow angle had struck the back of its head. The seared edges of a tear in his cooling cloak slumped over a killing wound the size of my hand. His occipital lobe had been vaporized in an instant. Gray powder drifted out of the wound and fear stirred deep in my subconscious. *That gray powder is his brain, is him—*

I sat in the dirt next to his corpse and took a deep breath. Purcell had ceased to exist when the laser sheared off the back of his head. He existed in my memory, no less now than he had the moment I'd heard of his disappearance decades prior. Whatever happened to this bundle of dry meat, shrunken skin, and desiccated brain could change nothing.

I pulled a DNA sampling kit from inside my cloak and scraped the collecting tip across his chest. I could identify him, but any greater victory was denied me. I knew what the red canyon had housed, but without the evidence lost with Purcell's missing subcutaneous data storage unit, I lacked any ability to prove it.

But Purcell had been killed! By human hands! Despite the USG's hegemony, that alone would be enough for an ALECS investigation committee to come back to Elard. I let the cameras in my contact lenses take in Purcell's mummified corpse. The tamper-proof time- and location-stamp would verify where and when I had seen this.

I sat for a moment, racking my memory for quotes from Marcus Aurelius or Laozi appropriate for commemorating a murder victim, then realizing my error. The world as it was had led him to violent death and a shallow grave, and led me to find him. The best I could do was set mantras aside and remember him, as he had been, and as he was.

Weighted down with solemnity, I stood, stretched my arms, turned my body, opened my eyes to look for Nesbitt's firing position—

Juliette stood a few meters away.

I looked to each side. If USG security wanted me dead or confined, it would have acted minutes ago. The desert terrain held only rocky soil and jumbled boulders. "Where are your friends?" I told her.

"I'm alone. USG doesn't know I'm here. Appel-Ball did me the same favor he did you."

I raised my eyebrow. "Clearly he didn't." A breeze stirred the loose sleeves of my desert cloak. "Why did you follow me?"

She stepped closer. Through the polarization of her face shield, her eyes implored. "Because I have to tell you something, before you leave tomorrow. I love you."

Anger washed like ice water down the inside of my chest. The wisdom of The Way chased it with pity, then calm. "You loved me so much you wanted me to leave for my safety. You thought better of an affair with me and sent me away to salvage your marriage. You're a nymphomaniac. Or nostalgia has you in its grip and I'm the only man from your younger days left here to ease it. I don't know what the true story is, and I do not care."

More steps brought her within a forearm's reach. She gripped my hand. My glove transmitted insistent warmth. "I'm so sorry I told you so many lies. I didn't know my own feelings for so many years. You were the man I should have chosen. Oh how I wish I'd known when you were still here—"

I pulled my hand from her grip. "You should have stuck with your first story. It was Nesbitt, wasn't it?"

"Nesbitt?"

I aimed my thumb over my shoulder. "Who killed Purcell."

Her eyes glistened. "You mean—?" Her lower lip curled.

"Take a look."

"Purcell's body. There. Killed." Her eyes looked glassy for a moment and I shifted my weight to catch her should she faint. She staggered back a step and leaned her hands on her knees. Her breaths rocked her torso. "How can you know he was killed?"

"A laser vaporized the back of his head. Take a look."

Juliette shut her eyes and breathed deeply. "I will," she said as she stood and sloughed out her breath. She went and crouched near Purcell's corpse.

I waited. After a time, she whispered a few words rendered indistinct by the rustle of our cloaks' cooling fans. A prayer, I assumed. For herself, not him.

Juliette stood and brushed dirt from her knees. "I didn't know. After Purcell disappeared, Nesbitt carried himself with a brooding mystery. He gave me the most dire looks when he thought I couldn't see. I realized he'd killed Purcell."

She only told half the truth. I stared back.

"I meant what I said to you. I wanted you to be safe. I didn't know I loved you, then, but I knew I didn't want you to die—"

"What was this place?"

Her brow crinkled. "What?"

"Jealousy had nothing to do with it. Nesbitt killed Purcell because he came here looking for something Nesbitt couldn't let him see. What was it?"

"What are you talking about?"

I gestured at the dwelling dug out of the canyon's far wall. "There's a dormitory and storehouse. Over there—" I pointed at the mound of spalled rock. "—is, well, perhaps you could tell me."

Her hands waggled in the air. "Some missionary field site. How should I know? Maybe Purcell came here to sketch and Nesbitt tracked him down."

"To sketch."

"Darren, he died with a pencil in his hand. Didn't you see?"

I subvoked, and my augmented reality hardware played video of Purcell's corpse on my contact lenses. She told a truth I hadn't noticed: a stubby pencil poked between withered fingers.

Why would he sketch the site below? Only video with an unforgeable time- and location-stamp would give Purcell the evidence he would have needed. A sketch would convince no one.

I remembered his sketchbooks. He never sketched to convince. He sketched to better understand what he saw. If what he saw ran counter to every ALECS protocol, then he might well have turned to a habit promising order and control over his inner world. It also explained why the sketch itself was gone. Nesbitt would have taken it for destruction, to close the final open loop.

I had as much evidence as I could find.

"He came out to sketch," Juliette said. Her tone, and the repetition, made the words more believable. "Nesbitt was jealous. Nesbitt followed him here and killed him. But now Nesbitt's dead too. It's just you and me. I know you have to leave tomorrow. My duty to the UCC means I have to stay. But we still have tonight. Let's spend it together so you can know I love you. How I wish I'd said it earlier, when we could have had a life together. But let's at least have one night, and a lifetime of memories."

I longed to believe her. Then I recalled the cut flaps of skin on Purcell's chest.

"You toyed with me," I said, "while your husband and your other lover played a game ending in death. All my memories of our intimacies—more than the sex. The sex was a tiny fraction. The emotional connections were far more important—are steeped in the wormwood of your motives. One night cannot cleanse those memories. Take care, Juliette. We shall never meet again."

She extended her hands. "There must be some way you can forgive me."

"I fell under your spell because I did not see the universe as it was. I cannot forgive myself."

I turned and stared into the red canyon. Time ticked by, counted by my deep and ragged breaths. A gust whistled through the vacant windows of the dwelling. Footsteps crunched on the rocky soil, grew quieter, faded from hearing. One last rustle of sound came from over a rise half a kilometer to the north. I looked up as her airmobile rose on a straight path toward the settlement.

I had evidence, but would it be anything more than a nuisance to USG? Before an ALECS investigation team could arrive, USG security would scrub the site and dismiss the data copied from my augmented reality sensors as fabrications. Give up. Let them win.

I took a centering breath. If USG had done what I suspected, I could not let it rest in its criminal victory. A few hours remained before I had to return to the settlement. What more evidence might still exist?

Sketches. Purcell might have made several drawings of the scene and Nesbitt might have missed one.... which the wind would have long since carried away, and Elar's harsh rays long since broken down its graphite streaks to dust.

Purcell's implanted hardware? Maybe he'd added a data chip to some other location in his body. Or Nesbitt had tried to destroy the hardware he'd cut out by smashing it against the rocks and been

incomplete. Hardware was more robust than most people thought...
and I still grasped at straws.

Yet I had no other chance of finding the evidence we would need, and
hours with nothing better to do. I trudged downslope to my airmobile,
pulled an object detector from a cargo bin, and returned to the boulders.

As I approached, I thought through Nesbitt's steps that day. He
had reached his firing position unseen by Purcell. If he had flown
directly from the settlement, he would have landed out of sight, just
as Juliette had, and returned to his vehicle by the same route. If he
had worked that day in the facility below, he would have looped wide
to stay out of Purcell's sight, but gone back straight downslope. He'd
been at the café with Juliette, Purcell, and me the night before, but I
hadn't seen him after about twenty-eight o'clock. Nesbitt might have
flown out here that night, or early the next morning, but how would
he know in advance Purcell's destin—

How many lies had Juliette told me, then and now?

I shook off the question. Perhaps Nesbitt had tailed Purcell from
the city and tracked him here. If Nesbitt had tossed aside a smashed
piece of implantable hardware on his way to his vehicle, it would be
between the boulder and his landing site. I would start along that
line, and if nothing turned up and I had time, I would check the slope
leading into the depression.

I stopped next to the boulder, then breathed into my abdomen
and started off. I soon developed a rhythm of detector sweeps. Draw a
line from the crevice to the small boulder I guessed to be Nesbitt's
firing position, go five meters to left and right of the line, find nothing,
step closer to the firing position, repeat. Doubt gnawed at me. Nesbitt
could have taken Purcell's implanted hardware back to USG headquarters for secure destruction. He could have thrown them ten
meters beyond the limit of my scan. I remembered an archaic joke, a
drunk on a nighttime sidewalk, looking for fallen keys—the physical
kind, metal with a jutting, notched shaft—but only in the light cone
cast by a streetlamp. *Over here, the light is better.*

The doubt kept gnawing as I worked my way from Nesbitt's firing position to Juliette's recent landing site. In truth, I had no idea where he might have landed. A dozen swells in the terrain could have hidden his landing from Purcell. My chances of success shrank with each step. Though Elar crept from the zenith toward the western horizon, like a sticky ball on a gentle slope, the shadows still grew longer.

I stopped amid the pattern of swirls her airmobile had left on the rocky soil. Nothing. My shoulders slumped. Forty-five minutes remained before I needed to return to the airfield. Not enough time to scour the slope in front of the boulders. But I would go until time ran out. I would sleep a little more soundly, recriminate myself a little less, in the days and weeks and months to come, if I looked as much as I could.

My detector had plenty of charge, so I left it on as I walked back to the boulder. I circled around to the right. Purcell had probably hidden in one of the low spaces between the boulder's underside and the wind-scooped dirt and rock. Which side of the boulder?

I knelt and craned my neck to look under the boulder. Against the shadowed rock, my camera picked up a spatter pattern. The detector's wand found the spatter enriched in iron, calcium, and L-amino acids. Nothing else.

Give it up, urged part of me. I checked the time. Five minutes before I needed to fly back to the settlement. Keep looking.

I went along the front of the boulder, then waved the detector at the other gap between the boulder and the ground. The detector squawked in my ear and dim smears of fluorescent green appeared in my field of vision, projected onto a low pile of dirt at the front of the gap.

The pile of dirt hid an object of plastic, metal, and glass, the latter just barely buried.

I crouched and clawed my gloved fingers at the rocky dirt. The smears in my field of vision grew more intense, more defined. I dug deeper, and struck something round and thin. I pulled on the object, scraped dirt with my fingers, pulled, scraped, then pulled it free.

A cracked plastic box barely big enough to hold a few petabytes of data. Two small lenses. Optical cables coupling the lenses to the box. I held the cables across my palm and let the box and cameras droop. A sudden fear of being seen whipped my head around. Only lifeless, rocky soil showed itself, and the cloudless sky held nothing but air.

I slipped the video recorder into my cooling cloak, then into a pocket of my cargo shorts. To my airmobile I hurried, pebbles scrabbling down with each step.

Two hours later, I returned to my flat. In the living room, I stepped past my half-packed luggage, checked the opacity of every window, and ran Clio's scanner over every surface.

Once convinced of my flat's security, I pulled the video recorder from my pocket and set it next to an induction charger. Despite the cracked housing, the ready light on the box flickered on, then glowed a steady green.

My augmented reality hardware interfaced wirelessly with the recorder. An authentication window popped into my vision. My chest tightened around my breath.

User: *wpurcell*

Password: |

Wherever I turned my head, the blinking cursor taunted me. Purcell seemed the type to use long alphanumeric strings of mixed case for his passwords. Given what he'd been looking for, he must have set the recorder to wipe after several failed logins.

I could let it go. Take the equipment back to Earth and let a data forensics expert in Calgary or Prague extract what could be gotten. But a part of me wanted to be certain what Purcell had found, and why Nesbitt had killed him.

I called Clio. "Could you come over? I need you to do something for me."

She blinked a few times. "*Daoshi*, you know we're packing up the last of the office today."

"Knowing Scobee, you finished in mid-afternoon."

"Well, yes, but I'm on duty until twenty o'clock, then those of us in the office are going for last drinks and dinner at that sushi box place on Gregory Dialogus—"

"You don't want to go there. Too many USG and UCC people."

She angled her head and dipped her chin to look up at me sidelong. "*Daoshi*, is it really necessary? Could it wait till the flight back?"

"No. I need you to do this as soon as you can."

Her head bobbed. "Of course, *Daoshi*. I'll see you about twenty-fifteen."

She arrived at the promised time. I hid the recorder in my pocket to mask any view a USG camera in the stairwell might see over her shoulder, then let her in. "Great to see you, Clio."

She hesitated at the threshold. "Are you sure we need to do this, *Daoshi*?"

I realized what she expected, then. "Absolutely," I said for the benefit of any hidden microphones. "But you have to come in."

The insistent tone from my baritone voice pulled her in. I shut and locked the door behind her. "Does USG security have bugs in the public spaces?"

"It does."

"With luck we sold them on this being an amorous encounter. Can you set the rattlers to send the same message out the windows? That should sell a cover story while we get to work."

Clio looked both relaxed and disappointed. "So what sort of security matter do you have for me?"

I pulled the recorder from my pocket. "It's password locked."

"They had passwords back then?" She lifted it up, ran her fingertip over the brittle plastic. "Where did you find this antique, *Daoshi*?"

"Out in the field. Its owner is long gone."

She squinted at a label on the underside, then blew away dust.

"Says its owner is The Unneeded Hypothesis. They had personnel here?"

"Decades ago. Around the time of my first posting. I'd like to spend my last night on Elard reminiscing about my first posting, and whatever video might be on here would help."

"You need me to live boot it?"

"However you can get me through the password lock."

She gave me a cautious look. "Are we going to cause an intra-ALECS incident?"

USG would never know— Not what she meant. "The Unneeded Hypothesis doesn't even know this recorder exists, let alone what might be on it." I quirked an eyebrow. "If you don't think you can crack it—"

"I can crack it, *Daoshi.*" Her eyebrows arched in return. "Was she a pretty woman?"

My head jittered, my eyes widened. Oh, she didn't mean Juliette. "Like I said, I don't know what video might be on there. I just want to find out. Nostalgia does funny things to someone my age."

She studied my face for a moment. "You don't seem so old as that, *Daoshi.*" She took the recorder and sat at the desk. I went to the kitchen for a glass of water. I needed to rehydrate after my day in the desert, and I wanted to keep my mind unfogged by alcohol. Through the door I glimpsed her profile as she worked. Stares at the box, fingers tapping keys on a virtual keyboard projected onto the desk by her augmented reality hardware, frowns at the wall. "He closed all the easy exploits, didn't he?" she muttered.

I downed the glass, poured another, let her work in peace.

After a time, she turned to me with a pleased look. "We're in, *Daoshi.*"

I went to the next room. I dug through the directory tree overlaid on my vision until I reached two video files, both the same length, about twenty minutes.

Clio said, "I'll go ahead and launch the viewer—"

"No. I'll take it from here. Go join the rest of the team for sushi boxes." I held my left hand behind her elbow, not touching, and gestured to the door with my right. Once she started that direction, I pocketed the recorder and followed. At the door, I reached around her for the knob—

"Not yet, *Daoshi.*" Her voice held an odd tone. She came closer and turned her face up to me. Her lips parted. "We have to sell it, right?"

I grasped her wrists and gently guided her forearms between us. "You will live a happy life with a good man." Gently but firmly, I said, "I'm not him."

She blinked, and allure melted from her features. Quickly, though, she saved face. "What I mean, *Daoshi,* is we need to—" She broke free of my grip and ruffled my hair. "—look the part."

"Yours too," I said. "And smudge your lipstick."

A few gyrations of her head disarrayed her hair. She nudged her mouth with the back of her hand. "Farewell, *Daoshi.* I'll see you at the spaceport tomorrow."

I shut the door behind her, then thumbed the lock. I hurried back to the desk and pulled the recorder from my pocket. Quick jabs of my finger at the air, and the videos started playing in tiled windows overlaid on my view of the wall.

The red canyon, looking toward the mound, looked similar to what I'd seen that afternoon. But the bone-white plugs in front of the mound held rigid metal frames about two meters tall. Hanging from the frames, rippling in a faint breeze, thin sheets of material bore the outline of a humanoid torso and head, each decorated with concentric circles.

Targets.

The other line of plugs walled off firing pits. The L-shaped remnant of foundation supported a building with walls open from a man's waist to the roof. Three men in USG security uniforms stood in the building, working at control panels just out of sight below the tops of the walls.

The USG security men looked toward the scarp, just as the other window showed individuals filing out of the barracks. A man at the front, a man at the end, and three men walking in cluster near the middle. One of the cluster, from his body language the leader, spoke with one of the line's eight natives. The latter wrinkled his snout and rolled his shoulders, gestures I recalled from my first arrival orientation as showing submission. The human leader took it in as if it were his birthright.

Every native, and the men at front and end of the column, carried a laser rifle.

The line of natives soon entered the firing pits. One of the men from the leader's cluster paced behind the firing pits, mouth moving and arms gesturing. A black box hanging on a lanyard around his neck was presumably a translation device. The recorder's microphone picked up a few indistinct words. English or a native language? I couldn't tell.

The next sights, and a few muffled sounds, removed all doubt. Capacitors crackled like distant firecrackers. Hazes of ablated target fabric and kicked-up dust came from the targets and the mound between them.

USG violated the core principles of ALECS.

Juliette must have known.

The video continued. Capacitors crackled. Dust hazes drifted up from the targets.

Another capacitor crackled, much louder.

The firing range fell still. The natives craned their necks and the men shaded their eyes with their hands as they looked toward the top of the slope. Agitation hunched their shoulders, until a few seconds later, the USG leader raised his hand in a question.

"Pest control," Nesbitt shouted a few meters from the recorder. I hadn't heard his voice for decades, but I knew it as if I'd heard it yesterday. "We can't let Terran life become an invasive species, right? Go back to work."

The USG leader nodded and gestured at his men and the native trainees. The firing range soon returned to normal.

The video ran on. After a while, the microphone picked up the sound of a nearby shovel biting the rocky soil.

Knuckles rapped on the door. I started. USG security? Had they outplayed Clio? I put the recorder into an unprotected sleep mode and hurried to the kitchen. A paper napkin, wadded as I walked back to the desk, thrown over the recorder—it would hide it enough if no one came in.

I slowed my steps and my breath as I neared the door. "Yes?"

"Darren."

What did Juliette want?

"I need to see you."

My heart thudded. I lifted my thumb toward the biometric lock and cursed myself as a fool before I opened the door a dozen centimeters.

"I'm still packing," I said. "I don't have much time."

Red rimmed her eyes. "Make the time. Please. You have to. I'll never see you again." She raised her hand to the outside of the door. Her fingertips brushed the nanofabbed wood.

I opened the door just wide enough to pull her in. I slammed and locked it before turning to her.

She started speaking before I fully faced her. "Are we alone?"

"I'm not hiding a lover in the bath—"

"Secure. Are we? You have to tell me."

"To the best of my knowledge."

She looked thoughtful for a moment. "USG security has no idea where you were today. Whoever on Scobee's staff is in charge of securing your facilities is well skilled." She exhaled and shivered. "Get us both a drink and meet me in the living room. I have to tell you the truth."

The poorly-masked recorder on the desk hovered in the corner of my eye. I kept my gaze on her. Part of me wanted to believe she meant what she said. "Have a seat."

I went to the kitchen and told the store'n'cook to make two strong martinis. With my back to the living room, I listened for her footsteps near the desk, and glanced that way every few seconds. She seemed to stay on the couch across the room until I returned with our drinks.

Juliette stared at the wall, her knuckles white on a clutch purse. She set the purse down to take her drink. She sipped from her glass and for long seconds her gaze watched the dance of room lights in the olive-tinged liquid. She took another sip before she spoke.

"It all began about nine months before Nesbitt killed Purcell.

"You wouldn't remember the night. We were in the old café on Gregory Dialogus. Purcell was always cynical about those of us who professed belief in something more than the universe's uncaring laws, but that night, after a few drinks, he was downright nasty. 'If Voltaire hadn't said it, he should have. Your UCC is neither Universal, nor a Church, nor of Christ.'"

"Sounds like Purcell," I said, "but you're right. I don't remember."

"Nesbitt was spoiling for a fight. Maybe he already intuited Purcell's suspicions. 'That's my wife you're insulting.'

"Purcell ignored him. He gave me that haughty look. 'Come now, Juliette, you know all that as well as I do. How often do your sermons mention Christ by name? Four times a year? You're more likely to celebrate your centuries of lesbian pastoresses who bravely protested every war the Americans ever fought, except those against Germans or white Southerners.'" She studied my face. "You still don't remember."

"Tense moments always popped up. Though more toward those last nine months."

"Of course, it would seem like any other. But when Nesbitt and I got home that night, we stayed up till three, talking about what Purcell might have already known and what he might find out."

"Might know—" The video of the firing range in use remained my secret. "—about?"

"USG sent Nesbitt out here to arm one tribe of natives with laser weapons."

"What?" With luck, I faked surprise well enough.

"USG headquarters on Earth had decided to reject the ALECS

standards of cooperation with other human organizations and non-interference with native cultural development. Elard was an experiment. USG would back some faction of natives, who would then make USG the sole human advisors on the planet. But USG was only willing to do it while maintaining plausible deniability. All the weapons were built on-planet, do you remember the first USG workshop out by the airfield? And if caught, Nesbitt would be denounced as a rogue by USG headquarters."

"What was your role? You meaning UCC, and you meaning... you."

"UCC headquarters didn't know about USG's plans when I married Nesbitt and it sent me here with him, but it did want to build a collaboration with USG. USG would pay lip service to our gospel of social justice, and we would preach a doctrine of 'render unto Caesar.' He didn't tell me his mission until a year after we arrived. But when he told me, he'd gauged me accurately. At the time. I agreed with him. It was God's plan to bring social justice to the Elard natives." She shook her head and a haggard look filled her eyes. "You can't make an omelet without breaking eggs, a million deaths are a statistic. Christ forgive me for thinking that."

"That's your judgment now," I said. "You were telling me about then."

"That night, I had a hunch Purcell had guessed something about USG's plans, and by three in the morning, Nesbitt agreed with me. Also that night, I realized how I could investigate Purcell."

The affair. "How did Nesbitt take *that*?"

"Do I look stupid? No man would accept his wife's suggestion to cheat on him. I kept quiet that night, and spent the next month dropping hints until he came up with the idea on his own. I put up enough sham resistance to make him think he had full control of the situation, then I 'went along' with his request."

A question came to mind. Did I really want to know the answer? Yes. "Where did I come in?"

"Deep down, Purcell was always aloof. His suspicions about

USG's and Nesbitt's activities made him even more wary of me when I started coming on to him. A sex addiction cover story was the best thing I could come up with. A few hookups here and there... a fling with you, and me arranging for Purcell to come across us in a compromising position...."

I breathed deep into my belly and held it for a five count. My emotions softened enough for me to think. "It worked."

Juliette crinkled her face and avoided my gaze. "Like I knew it would. A few days later Purcell let me into his flat—"

A part of me exulted that I had taken pleasure from her flesh before Purcell.

"—and within a month, I knew all his secrets. I wriggled out from his arm as he snored and flipped through his sketchbooks until I found the map."

She met my gaze then. "How did you find it? I destroyed what I thought was the only copy five minutes after Nesbitt called me from the training facility to tell me he'd killed Purcell. And we cracked Purcell's computer security and found no electronic copies."

"I have my ways. So Purcell had evidence pointing to a few different sites out in the desert, and he sneaked off to spy on each one in turn. He didn't realize how well you were tracking him. When he went to the red canyon, Nesbitt followed him."

"And you know what happened next."

"Why have you told me this?"

In passing, a swallow of her martini bulged her neck. "Because Nesbitt and I were evil and I have to atone somehow. We violated our ALECS vow. We sent tens of thousands of natives to their deaths. We lied to Purcell and we killed him."

All true. But. "What triggered your change of heart?"

Juliette turned her gaze to the floor. In her eyes welled tears. Perhaps the first honest ones she'd ever cried in front of me. "I meant every word I said at the red canyon. I'm alone. While Nesbitt lived, I off-loaded my conscience to him. His end justified all our means. But after he died—and he was killed fighting native rebels holding out against the Indigenous Autonomous Council, you guessed that already?—I couldn't deny my responsibility any more."

More tears welled in her eyes. Juliette threw her arms around me and burrowed against my chest. I returned the embrace and held her close for a time. Choked-back sobs spasmed through her torso, and her breath came fast and ragged, but she did not cry. Her breaths slowed and her body relaxed. I kept holding her close.

She looked up at me. Her face was composed despite the red of uncried tears like a mask around her eyes. "Take me."

"Juliette—"

"Give me this. If you want to think of it as revenge for how I used you, think that. I would deserve it. But you're the only man alive I ever might have loved and ever could love and after tomorrow I'll never see you again. Give me this."

She reached up to the back of my head and pulled my mouth toward hers. I resisted for a few seconds, but then the warmth of her lips and the memory of our long-ago trysts stiffened my penis and I chose to give her what she wanted.

I walked her backwards to the bed. Moments later our clothes fell to the floor. I attended to her pleasure, but when the time came to take mine, I held her wrists to her pillow and pounded my body against hers. Her hips soon rocked in time with mine.

Afterward, we lay next to each other, catching our breaths and letting our sweat dry, I thought of the sleeping recorder under the napkin in the next room. Was that enough? If USG could muddy the water, with accusations of forgery and lies, could it escape the punishment it deserved?

"If you want to fully atone for Nesbitt's crimes, come to the spaceport tomorrow."

Sadness returned to her eyes. "Don't say that."

"If the ALECS Executive Committee had your testimony, USG would be crushed—"

"Darren, don't you see? I can't leave Elard. I know too much."

Gooseflesh covered my cheeks and neck. I should have already known.

She went on without noticing my reaction. "USG security would stop me before I got to the departure gate. And they would stop you too. They might let me live, but you? I can't let them do that to you. I already sent Purcell to his death. Don't ask me to send you to yours."

"There has to be a way," I said. "We could smuggle you on-board somehow."

"I'm not petite enough to fit in someone's luggage."

"We could nanofab a life support crate overnight and have Scobee declare it privileged—"

"Does The Way in the West have its own private assemblery? No? USG would know what you nanofabbed. They would scan it despite the privilege. And Scobee's blood would be on my hands too." She lifted her hand to my cheek. "I can't leave. You must. You have to find a way to expose what USG did here. That, and my memories of tonight, will be enough for me. Let them be enough for you."

We could disguise her and give her false papers as a member of The Way in the West... and USG had a list of every one of our members still on Elard and could take DNA from her to hunt for matches in the ALECS personnel database.

Next plan. We could....

I let out a long breath. She was right. If she tried to leave, USG security would stop her, and then stop me. The evidence I had from Purcell's camera would have to be enough to bring about justice.

"They are," I said.

We lay for a time, the only sounds our breaths and the rush of cooled air through the vents. Eventually I fell asleep.

An alarm clock blatted. I stopped it, then lurched awake.

Juliette was gone.

A message from her bounced on the bottom of my vision until I subvoked it open. *My memories of last night are so powerful, I couldn't risk my saying something to spoil them. Perhaps you feel the same. Take care. J.*

Disappointed, I shook my head. I had an hour before I needed to leave for the spaceport. No time to ponder her flightiness. Showering, dressing, packing Purcell's recorder—

I scrambled into the living room. The napkin tossed over the recorder was still there, but what was underneath—?

The recorder. It remained in power-save mode. After a few breaths, I carried it back to the bedroom and stuffed it into my attaché case.

By nine o'clock, robots had loaded my luggage into my jitney. I started down the street toward Guru Nanak Boulevard. The boulevard held more traffic this morning than I had seen over all daylight hours of the last month. People squeezed by fives and sixes into jitneys and robots packed and repacked luggage into the cargo compartments. USG security personnel in black cloaks and opaque face shields stood at major intersections, laser rifles slung over their shoulders. Traffic crawled past their unreadable gazes.

My jitney sped up as we neared the exit of the settlement proper. The air curtains remained, but USG security had broadcast an all-clear appearing as a green icon in my field of vision. A glimpse at the gatehouse showed two security men with relaxed poses and crossed arms chatting to themselves.

At the spaceport, a robotic cart and the envious looks of people dragging their luggage waited for me. Rank had its privileges. Anxious faces and bickering couples surrounded me. Only the few USG personnel returning to Earth showed anything resembling delight, tinged with the cruelty of boys not yet grown up.

Eventually I reached the line for the security checkpoint. At the head of the line stood a gray plastic frame, two meters fifty tall, one meter fifty wide, thirty centimeters thick. I shuffled along with the queue. The morose faces around me repelled any urge of mine for small talk.

At my turn, the guard gestured at the brain activity scanner. I waited on the outlines of feet, breathing deep and trying not to think of the previous day and night.

The guard squinted at my passport while motors and fans in the scanner whirred at high speed. "What was the purpose of your visit, *Daoshi* Lee?"

"Supervising the withdrawal by The Way in the West of its personnel and assets from Elard."

"Hmm." He peered at some detail shown by the brain activity scanner. "What's in your luggage?"

A chill stole over my neck. "My personal effects," I said in an off-hand tone. Think of Juliette. Think of last night, in bed, after we talked on the couch in the living room near the desk—

"The Indigenous Autonomous Council has forbidden the export of native artifacts and recordings of cultural performances."

The natives in the firing pits in the red canyon. I called up memories of Juliette's body as quickly, held them as firmly, as I could. "I haven't seen a native this entire trip," I said.

Two more USG security personnel came toward the scanner and stopped between me and the concourse leading to the departing ship. The guard at the scanner's control panel cleared his throat. "These men will guide you to a lounge while we check your luggage. It shouldn't take but an hour."

"It had best not. If I'm held here against my will out of some power-trip of yours, the ALECS Executive Committee will have much to ask your masters about."

The guard gave me a flat look. "If all is in order, you'll be on board well before launch."

One of the security men led me away from the concourse to the ship. The other fell in behind me. Part of me longed to sprint away from the guards and toward the ship. A rabbit or squirrel might feel the same, when a trap snared its leg. But flight would do no good. Even if I made it to the ship, USG's security personnel could deny the ship freedom to launch until they found me.

A door unsealed itself and we descended an echoing stairwell. Without a word, the security men showed me a small lounge containing two ugly armchairs and stark white light. I squinted and sat. In an animated poster on the wall in front of me, Vainqueur posed with members of the Indigenous Autonomous Council. I crossed my arms over my chest to try to hide my heart's slamming.

If Clio had been able to crack the recorder's password protection, couldn't USG?

I took deep breaths and meditated on a native's cooling crest. The exercises calmed me enough to think how I might talk myself out of their discovery of the data.

I found that old thing, oh, that's what was on it?

There are a hundred copies on board the ship already, and you can't arrest everyone before departure time.

Am I going to have break cover and call Vainqueur?

More deep breaths. What a mediocre set of cover stories. Still more deep breaths—

The two USG security personnel knocked before coming in. "You're free to go," one said. "We'll lead you back to the concourse and you can find your way to the ship from there."

"That's it? Where's my apology?"

The second USG man frowned. "You mean, the apology you owe us, for thinking we're drones of some police state when you go through the scanner?"

After a tense silence, the first one said, "Follow us."

A few minutes later, I stood alone on the concourse with the robotic cart holding my luggage. My legs wobbled the first steps toward the ship. How had I eluded them? Had Juliette gotten my name onto a whitelist? I clamped my face over feelings of relief and good fortune.

At the end of the concourse, the robot lifted my luggage onto the conveyor leading to the ship's complement of cargo handlers. I opened my eye and pressed my thumb for the biometric scanners and a small chip with my stateroom assignment clacked out.

Ten minutes later, my luggage all stowed in my stateroom, I fell back on the bed and shivered. I had dodged a bullet. Once we lifted off, nothing could touch me. Within a day of my return to Earth, the

ALECS Executive Committee would have a copy of Purcell's evidence.

A dark intuition snapped open my eyes. I lunged for my luggage.

Clio's hack of the recorder's login responded to my biometrics. Heart thudding, I checked the directory tree.

The recorder's images had been wiped.

For some long time, I couldn't move, couldn't even think. When my thoughts finally did flow, they bobbed along a sea of anger. *How could she have done this? Miserable lying—*

She saved your life—

'Don't bother asking, "Why were such things made in this world?"'—

I threw away the bitter cucumber. I had lost the most valuable evidence I'd found. That couldn't be helped. What evidence remained? A sample of Purcell's DNA. What I had seen. What I had heard. The latter two items backed up on a datachip.

She could have destroyed it too.

I went to my attaché and pulled out a gray datachip case with a biometric lock. I sagged into a chair and my hands trembled as I thumbed the lock and pushed open the lid. The case sprang open to reveal two datachips.

Two?

I subvoked to my augmented reality hardware, then held the second datachip close to my chest for a low-latency connection. A window appeared in my vision.

User: dlee

Password: |

I stared at the blinking cursor for a moment, before the obvious password occurred to me. A virtual keyboard appeared across my thighs. I typed *juliette.*

A file browser opened. At the root of the datachip's directory tree I found several folders and a file named VIEWME.

I opened the file. A video window popped up, overlaid to the right of a closet door on the stateroom wall.

Juliette in her living room. Alphanumerics in the lower right timestamped the recording at about two hours after she met me at Purcell's corpse.

Come to gloat? I extended my arm to backhand the video window into the trash. But another, calmer part held me back.

"Hello Darren. If you're still on Elard, stop watching now. All I'm going to do is reminisce about our affair in the old days." Haunted eyes belied her words for three slow beats of my heart.

"I assume you're past the brain activity scanners. USG on Elard cannot stop you from getting to Earth. You might not thank God you're safe, but let me thank Him for you." Her eyes grew moist. "I wish I could have met you before Nesbitt. But all I can do is choose you now, when I'm a prisoner who knows too much and you're the one chance I have to reveal USG's crimes. You're the one chance I have to atone for my role in those crimes. Go, to Earth, and live."

She lifted the datachip I now held. "I copied all Nesbitt's files right after he died, before USG security scrubbed all his sensitive data from our flat. I held onto them in case this chance might come. Use them wisely.

"Good-bye, Darren. Know you go with all the love I'm capable of giving."

The video stopped and the window shut itself. For a few seconds, I stared at the now-blank wall where her face had been shown. Then I navigated through the files she had copied.

Perhaps not all Nesbitt's files, but thousands, with created and modified dates spanning decades. I skimmed them while heeding the pre-launch instructions from the ship with half my mind. Strategy papers from USG headquarters. Video from the first laser rifle fab out by the airfield. Logs of personnel working in weapons fab and native military training. Maps of the firing range in the red canyon, and others Purcell had never known about. Video of natives posing with energy weapons.

Far away, the fusion drives rumbled to life, and acceleration pushed me into the launch couch.

I barely noticed. I kept reviewing the files. Nesbitt's reports, dozens of them, with frank description of military training of his native allies, their combat operations against other native factions.

His killing of Purcell.

Twenty minutes later, the ship announced we could unstrap from our launch couches. I copied the files to my other datachip and to a memory implanted under my skin, then sealed Juliette's datachip back in the case.

I left my stateroom and asked the ship to guide me to Scobee and Clio.

ABOUT THE AUTHOR

I'M **RAYMUND EICH.** I use my Middle American upbringing as a launchpad for journeys to the ends of the Universe.

Growing up in the Midwest prepared me for my academic career, culminating with a Ph.D. in biochemistry from Rice University. It helps me help inventors prosper from their progress in medicine, biotechnology, and computer hardware.

Above all, it inspires me to write science fiction and fantasy about ordinary people facing extraordinary wonders and horrors, battling enemies both foreign and domestic, and building better lives for themselves, their families, and their societies.

My last name has one syllable and is pronounced "eye-sh." I live in Houston with my family.

Connect with me at **www.raymundeich.com** or follow the QR code below.

————

Online and brick-and-mortar bookstores around the world list millions of books, with thousands more published every day. I'm glad you discovered this one.

If you'd like to know when I release a new book, instead of leaving it to chance, join my Readers Club. I'll email you from time to time with publishing news, off-beat patents, a short personal update, or a reminder about an older book of mine you might have missed.

Yes, please! I'll go to **www.raymundeich.com/mailing-list** or scan the QR code below.

No thanks. I'll take my chances next time I look for your books.

OTHER BOOKS BY THE AUTHOR

Available wherever books are sold.

Learn more about these titles at our website, **www.cv2books.com,** or follow the QR code below.

THE FALSE FLAG WAR

Concordia's mission reflected the best of the human race. Crew and scientists from both of Earth's rival factions, Humanists and Traditionalists, journeyed for years at relativistic speeds to reach Bravo Charlie, a life-bearing planet orbiting Alpha Centauri B, to expand the frontiers of knowledge for all.

Concordia's mission also reflected humanity at its worst. Corrupt bureaucrats and ambitious political leaders in both factions maintained a status quo backed by weapons of mass destruction. The faction commanders on the mission each sought to seize advantages for their side alone.

Then the ship received transmissions. Signs of an ancient, powerful alien presence on the planet below.

Exploration 2127

Sent to explore, **Jaeger** and **McIlroy**, born and raised in a Texas divided by razor wire and minefields. Men torn between the mission's ideals and orders from their respective faction commanders, oily Varanathan and domineering Sandford.

Then Jaeger and McIlroy discover how to bring Earth's factions together... using knowledge given by aliens dead over a million years.

Invasion 2132

Concordia fell silent. Mission control now detects an unknown ship leaving the Alpha Centauri system. Heading to Earth at relativistic speeds. Silent about its purpose. Its crew unknown.

Earth's one chance: Its rival factions must work for mutual defense. While shadowy figures strive to use the unknown ship for their own faction's gain.

STONE CHALMERS

Earth barely survived the 21st Century.

Biotechnological and nuclear terrorism, civil war, famine, and ethnic cleansing killed billions. Thousands fled on warpdrive ships to colonize planets around distant suns.

In the 22nd century, after Earth unified under one world government, it opened wormhole links to the distant colonies, to prevent a repeat of the previous century's chaos on a galactic scale.

Enter operative Stone Chalmers. Spy. Assassin. Instrument maintaining Earth's dominion over all human worlds.

Opposing him are hostile forces on colony worlds... and within the Earth government itself.

When Stone clashes with those forces, Earth—and every human world—will be transformed forever.

Learn more about the Stone Chalmers series at
www.cv2books.com/stone-chalmers, or follow the QR code below.

The Progress of Mankind

To maintain order in the 22nd century, Earth relocates undesirables through artificial wormholes onto colony planets. Everyone benefits… except the planets' original colonists.

Now, the newly rediscovered colony of New Moravia learns Earth's plan and fights back.

The Greater Glory of God

Thousands fled the chaos of the 21st century on rogue warpdrive ships to settle colony planets. When Earth reunified in the 22nd, its fleets rediscovered the colonies and hunted down the warpdrive ships.

Every warpdrive ship but one.

To All High Emprise Consecrated

Unified Earth has rediscovered the colony of Minerva. Prosperous and technologically advanced, Minerva quickly submits to Earth supremacy.

Surprisingly quickly…

In Public Convocation Assembled

Earth's government controls all human colonies scattered through the galaxy by means of wormholes, warpdrive ships, and ruthless operatives. Operatives working to strengthen Earth's grip.

Or destroy it.

THE CONFEDERATED WORLDS

The purpose of all other combat arms is to put the infantryman in sole possession of the battlefield.

A thousand years from now, while Earth sleeps in virtual reality, three polities—the Confederated Worlds, the Unity, and the Progressive Republic—strive to connect the scattered, terraformed worlds of humankind by artificial wormholes.

When they meet, they clash, in a decades-long struggle of arms that will embroil every human world, in which dedication to duty liberates worlds—and oneself.

Learn more about the Confederated Worlds series at **www.cv2books.com/the-confederated-worlds**, or follow the QR code below.

Take the Shilling

The Confederated Worlds implanted in his brain the skills to make him a soldier. Tomas Neumann had to learn for himself how to survive interstellar war.

Operation Iago

The Confederated Worlds lost the war. Can Lt. Tomas Neumann win the peace against elusive, deceptive foes out to turn the Confederated Worlds against itself?

A Bodyguard of Lies

Assigned to the halls of power, only Capt. Tomas Neumann can save the Confederated Worlds from the ultimate treachery.

OTHER NOVELS

The Blank Slate

Neuroscience entrepreneur Clay Shieffer must stop a tyrannical president... because he unwittingly gave the tyrant power over the human mind.

New California

After New California's founder committed suicide, two men vied to rule the colony.

Ashwin George, supported by the colony's elite and the Chinese company dominating half the settled galaxy.

Against him, Desmond Park, nanotechnology engineer, armed with the most formidable weapon of all.

A single idea.

The Reincarnation Run

Skeptical spacejock Landry Krieger knows exactly how to smuggle the "reborn" spiritual leader of an oppressed people past their conquerors... but the boy's priests—and governess—shake up his orderly plans.

Azureseas: Cantrell's War

Ross Cantrell joined the animal control mission on the newly-discovered planet Azureseas to earn the money to start married life together with his girlfriend.

Then Ross discovers the truth about the planet's "animals."

SHORT NOVELS

A Mighty Fortress

Theodore and his team from the Lutheran Interstellar Terraforming Society would transform a barren, rocky world into a refuge of faith and life.

Or die trying.

Winner and the Poacher

A Portia Oakeshott, Dinosaur Veterinarian Short Novel

As a consultant to law enforcement, Portia confronts stark evidence of a rich young man's crime: the mounted head of a massive herbivorous *Wintonotitan*. A winner.

A dinosaur the company never granted a permit for hunting.